GOLDEN VALLEY

GOLDEN VALLEY

A NOVEL OF CALIFORNIA

BY FRANCES GRAGG AND
GEORGE PALMER PUTNAM

G7586 g

DUELL, SLOAN AND PEARCE · New York

The creation and the writing of Golden Valley owes much to Ralph Bandini whose enthusiasm for the story contributed much to its ultimate publication.

G. P. P.

GOLDEN VALLEY

Chapter 1.

As I finally came downstairs that morning, my granddaughter Abby was waiting, sprawled inelegantly in a taffy-colored chair sipping a glass of milk, sombrero and gauntlets on the floor beside her.

With one lithe movement she was on her feet, her arms around me.

"Here you are at last!" she exclaimed. "I thought you'd never wake up."

As she stood back, holding my hands in hers, I was struck afresh with the girl's loveliness. Abby was half a head taller than I, slim as a boy, tanned and ruby-lipped. The bright Inyo sunshine flooding the room caught up the lights in her hair, but not even our Sierra sky could match the blue of her eyes. She wore her divided skirt of fringed buckskin, a white blouse with cowboy's cravat of red, and high-heeled boots.

"It was a weary journey."

"But you got what you went after."

I nodded dubiously. It was only on the previous day's long drive up from Mojave that the enthusiasm of our friends almost overwhelmed us. While John and I had been in Washington, the engineers actually had appeared though we in truth knew nothing of it. And then suddenly the whole country seemed sure that at last the reclamation of our valley's thirsty acres would commence.

"Why, Hanny!" Abby chided. "You *look* as if you had doubts."

"Well, child. . . ." I kissed her. "There is one certainty with no question at all. I'm wonderful glad to be home again."

"It's mighty nice to have you, ma'am." She curtsied lightly.

"At least it's a good thing for me to go away once in a while," I continued, as she sat herself on the arm of my chair. "It makes me appreciated. And," I added, patting her slim brown hand, "it helps me realize how beautiful you are."

"Now what are you after?" Abby chuckled. "We're alike as two peas, and you know it. I've heard that all my life." She took hold of my shoulders, raised me from the chair, and turned me about to face the French mirror hanging on the far wall.

There I was, a light, rather brittle woman with gray hair, whiting at the temples, a skin still clear but having no longer the firmness of youth, eyes a little faded, a little tired, with tiny wrinkles at their corners, a mouth set in lines of sorrow as well as laughter. I shook my head. " 'Alike as two peas.' Absurd!"

4

As Abby stood for a long moment, I saw a gleam light her eyes. "You stay right here till I come back," she commanded, and ran toward the stairs.

Mildly curious, I went into the kitchen. Gim Lee was nowhere in sight. I poured my coffee and took it back into the sitting room, sinking into my favorite rocker by the window.

As I sat in that pleasant house of ours, so different from the log cabin it had grown from, and the first house of sod, my eyes traveled to the High Sierra, the great barrier guarding the valley we'd come to forty years before. The smooth granite, as the sun struck it, shone white as snow. Venturesome pines and juniper darkened the cleft canyons where there was any foothold at all. A thunderhead was piling up behind the jagged skyline; soon there would be rain on top. Then the mountain meadows would take on a fresh-washed green, the somber trees would seem to lift a little toward the sky. In imagination I could hear the streams chuckling as they joined together on their journey to meet the lines of brown willows that threaded up from the valley. These same waters, come so far from so high, in rivulets and ditches we had made criss-crossed our own acres and the lands of our neighbors, and seeped up from below to make green the fields that were not actually reached by the captured surface waters.

Water was indeed the life's blood of our country. And now at last all that precious treasure which wasted each season was to be put to its full use as we had dreamed some day would be done.

My eyes moved from the emerald fields—it was easy

to remember when they had been gray sagebrush—to the trees that bordered them, those proud poplars John had planted in this land where there were no trees at all. It seemed such a short time since that bitter spring when the frosts had killed the first of them and John had brought more from the little valleys of the foothills, and these had lived and grown straight and tall, the symbol of our home-site my husband loved best.

Then my reverie ended as I heard a quick step, and looking up I caught my breath. Standing on the stairs was a vision from the yesterdays of my youth. A figure with lifted head in my old black velvet gown with the polonaise and high, fluted lace collar. My cameo brooch was at the throat, the hair arranged in the old fashion, high in front with little curls brought down the neck to complement the gown. One hand rested lightly upon the banister, the other was laid against the slim throat just below the brooch.

As I stared, speechless, the hand lifted gracefully and on the wrist was my old bracelet of heavy beaten gold. I rose from my chair as though lifted by invisible hands. My knees were trembling a little. Then the figure rushed toward me with a great rustling of petticoats and Abby was laughing down into my astonished face.

"I did startle you, didn't I?" she cried, triumphantly. "And I am just like you, aren't I? I tried it the other day, Hanny, and Grampy looked at me as if he'd seen a ghost."

The sight of this young girl in my old finery left me breathless.

"I told you we were alike as two peas," Abby rattled on, preening before the French mirror as her mother had done at her age. "I've rummaged until I've found all your beautiful things. When I put them on I make believe I *am* you, years and years ago, when you first saw Golden Valley." Her eyes darkened as she widened them. "I can see it all when I'm dressed this way. Big, lonely, empty. Miles and miles of gray sageland. Lines of brown willows coming down from the mountains. Two wagons, just little specks, crawling southward. It's fun, Hanny!"

The clamor of the knocker averted any reply I might have made, and Abby whirled about and stepped to the door in her rustling skirts.

A tall young man stood on the threshold, dressed in worn khaki, his trousers stuffed into the tops of surveyor's boots. His jaw dropped and he made no attempt to speak as he stared at Abby.

"Good morning," I said. "Won't you come in? I am Mrs. Weston, and this is my granddaughter, Abby Cabot." I smiled at her consternation. "She has dressed herself like this to show me how I used to look. Won't you come in?"

The young man flushed, and I saw that Abby's cheeks were pink, too, as she snatched her hand from the door-knob and backed into the room, her eyes going helplessly toward the stairs.

The young stranger found his voice, a very pleasant one. "Thank you," he said. "I am David Allen." Since my own David had gone, the name always brought a little constriction to my throat. He went on, becoming more at ease as he talked. "I've a surveying crew. We're camped up the creek a way."

I took the peaked Stetson he held. If he was in charge

7

of a surveying crew it undoubtedly meant that he was employed by the government in connection with its new reclamation project that had burst upon us so suddenly. Named David, a government engineer—what better introduction could he bring?

"Won't you have some coffee?" I asked. "I'm taking my ease this morning. I've just returned from the East. In the meantime"—I glanced at Abby with a twinkle—"my granddaughter can change."

"Of course," Abby laughed a little breathlessly, "I—I hope you don't think I'm crazy!" she shot at our visitor.

"Crazy?" He looked at her appraisingly. "If you are, I think I like insanity." His smile was ready, with a certain eagerness. "You did stop me a bit when you opened the door in that outfit. You see, I had no idea of crashing into a page of history—especially so beautifully illustrated."

Abby dropped an old-fashioned curtsey.

"Matter of fact, I just came to buy a few bales of hay."

"Oh," said Abby. Then she added with a giggle, "You and Hanny work out the hay deal while I go find some civilized clothes." She gathered her skirts and ran up the stairs.

I motioned David Allen to a chair and sat down beside him.

"You wanted to buy some hay?" I asked.

"Well, yes, ma'am. You see, we have some horses and we're likely to be camped where we are for quite a while. We've got a spring wagon and could attend to the hauling. . . ."

I smiled. "We're rather partial to surveyors these days."

8

He looked faintly puzzled, but said at once, "Then you think it could be arranged?"

"I'm sure of it. I'll speak to Mr. Weston about it tonight."

The more I looked at this caller the better I liked him. He was not particularly handsome. But he was tall, lean-jawed, and steady of gaze, and his face as well as his well-knit body had a look of strength that I liked. His hands pleased me, too—long-fingered and calm; I could never abide to see a man fidget. He was tanned nut-brown, and his hair was dark and a little unruly.

We heard Abby's step on the stairs, and David Allen was on his feet. She was in her riding clothes again.

"Any more tricks up your sleeve?" he teased, his admiring look clinging to her face.

I slipped out for the coffee I had offered the visitor, and when I returned he and Abby were chatting animatedly. Young Allen had graduated from the University of California and had been at Berkeley during the two years Abby attended Mills College. I crept unobtrusively to my rocker and listened to their revelations. They could not understand, it seemed, how they had never met—there being no more than several hundreds of thousands of people living in and about the Bay District.

"D'you happen to know Mary Sturgiss?"

"Johnny Charles?" he laughed. "You mean old Mush! Say, look here, Miss Cabot, where did you keep yourself anyway. . . ."

"I'll never understand how we missed each other," Abby exclaimed at last.

"I'm not going to waste time trying," David Allen answered seriously. "I like it the way it happened better—me knocking at the door this morning, looking for a bale of hay, and there you were all dressed up like a fancy valentine. Knocked the hay clean out of my mind! Well, ma'am"—he turned to me with an engaging smile—"then may I count on getting that hay?"

"Of course," I assured him.

When he had thanked me, he turned again to Abby. "I do hope I can see you again soon?"

There was such urgency in his voice that somewhat to my surprise, I found myself saying, "Won't you have dinner with us next Saturday night?" From the look on her face I was half afraid Abby might have asked him for that very night. "Say, six o'clock?"

"I'll be delighted, ma'am," he accepted eagerly. "*You'll* be here?" he added, turning to Abby.

Abby had the grace to blush but answered unhesitatingly, "Yes. I nearly always am. Ask Hanny!"

Abby and I stood together in the hall as he took his leave, Abby looking intently at the blank white surface of the door after it had closed. I could hear the faint clinck of silver spoons against china, and knew Gim Lee was slipping about the sitting room, gathering up our soiled cups. I turned and Abby, emerging from her sudden dream, followed me. For several minutes she busied herself at imaginary tasks. A picture that had always hung right before suddenly needed to be straightened. A doily was picked up and laid meticulously down again in exactly the same place; some dust I could not see, brushed from the table. And all the while Abby kept her back turned.

It seemed to me that I loved her more in that strained moment than ever before. Then, without any warning, she rushed to my chair and dropped on her knees, burying her face in my lap.

"Oh, Hanny!" she gasped softly from the folds of my dress.

"Yes, child? What is it, Abby dear?" I bent over and kissed the bright hair.

"What *is* it, Hanny? What's the matter with me?"

Marking time myself, now, I gently stroked her hair. Its silken fineness clung to my touch.

"Suppose you tell me, Abby," I said.

"I—I don't know how, Hanny," she whispered. "I. . . . Did you like him?" I could tell she was holding her breath for my answer. I couldn't help wondering how much it would have mattered if I hadn't liked him.

"Yes," I replied promptly. "I liked him very much."

"Liked him. . . ." Abby gave a little laugh. "Do you— do you believe there's really such a thing—outside of books, I mean—as love at first sight?" I felt her burrowing deeper, keeping her hot face out of my sight.

I sat very still, thinking of the time I first laid eyes on John Weston. How I had trembled inwardly, felt afraid and enchanted all at once. . . .

"Yes, child," I said firmly, "I do."

It was after five when John came home, his eyes eager, his head erect. The years had dealt kindly with my husband; his hair was less gray than mine, and though his waistline had thickened, the proudness of his bearing as

11

he came toward me might have been that of a man of thirty-five.

As I looked at him, thinking this, he caught me up in his arms and swung me about gleefully.

"It's true, Abbie girl!" he chortled, setting me back on my feet.

"Well," I gasped, "don't forget it's also true you're a grandfather."

"And behave as such, eh?" John chuckled, cocking his head to one side the way he'd always done when he was primed with good news.

"That might be appropriate," I said primly, patting my hair back in place. Then I laughed. "Now you tell me."

"Great news, Abbie. About the best we've ever had. The government's moved in. Opened an office in Bishop. A government engineer named Enderby is in charge. Field crews are out. They're going to start at Bishop, then work on down. Big Pine, Independence, Lone Pine. Maybe Olancha—I don't know about that. But it's big, Abbie, the biggest thing that's ever happened to us."

John strode to the window to stare out at the mountains, the orchards, his own row of beloved tall trees.

"Everybody's riding on air. Paul Gideon's talking of enlarging his store. Frank Masters tackled me about buying some stock in his bank." He grinned at me with a raised eyebrow. "He wasn't so pleased when I put him off."

Frank Masters was likable and generous, a good friend, too. But his banking methods were too free and easy to suit John and me. For that reason we kept the bulk of what money we had in San Francisco's Wells-Fargo Nevada

12

Bank, and felt a little ashamed of it. One couldn't blame Frank for wanting to expand now.

"Everything all right here?" John finally asked. "Reclamation or no, we've got to keep the ranch going."

"Everything's all right," I answered. "So Gim Lee says, and you know he knows everything that's going on. I've been busy, too. Abby's husband-to-be was here." I rocked placidly. John was not to have all the triumphs of that day.

His reaction was explosive. "What are you talking about?" he demanded.

"Abby's future husband," I repeated. "A government engineer by the name of Allen. If I'm any judge, he took our Abby's heart right out that door with him. He's coming for dinner, next Saturday."

"You're not just romancing?"

I assured him that I was not and proceeded to go over the happenings of the morning in detail, finding a curious pleasure in the telling as I watched John's perplexed face.

Then he grinned. "Love at first sight, eh?"

I said that that was it exactly.

"You're sure," he teased me, "you haven't been reading too many old-fashioned novels?"

"Some fashions just don't change."

"That could be. Perhaps even in this year of the Lord 1910 we're not as modern as we might be." Then a scowl of puzzlement clouded John's face. "Maybe you know what you're talking about."

"You'd be sure if you'd seen what I saw."

John shook his head. "I mean the young fellow—not Abby. He's the puzzle." He flung out of his chair, pacing

13

the floor. "What gets me is the government being down here already. None of the ranchers seem to know that. I'll set them by their ears tomorrow!" He turned to me, his eyes crinkling. "Says he wants hay? Give it to him. All he wants. Give him the ranch if he wants it!"

"Abby, too?" I suggested lightly.

"Well. . . ." he demurred, "he'll have to be a *very* good reclamation engineer to deserve that!"

Chapter 2.

*S*LEEP would not come to me. Altogether too much had happened on that day which seemed the threshold of such infinitely promising tomorrows. And tomorrow and today were so close to the yesterdays that had created them—the yesterdays of my memories.

I slipped into my dressing gown and, shading my old oil lamp in my hand, went out from our bedroom to the little sewing alcove we had built atop the verandah, a cozy place with windows that gave out onto the mountains and desert. The clean breath of sagebrush scented the air. Backdrop for my remembering towered the Sierra Nevada, vague and shadowed against the pale sky. There, for a long hour of that long night I lived again those yesterdays which John and I had shared and which were the deep foundations for whatever lay in store for us and for our valley.

Minersville was a dismal place. John worked then in a mine for ten dollars a day, paid in gold dust, but with potatoes two dollars the pound, and eggs twenty-five cents each, the money scarcely bought plain provisions. I managed to make both ends meet by washing clothes for the miners, making sometimes as much as twenty-three dollars a day; but the heavy red flannels were hard to handle, and my hands cracked and bled from the work and the weather.

It was there that I first heard about Inyo from the Wagnells. They had just come from that great valley between high snow-capped mountains. Mrs. Wagnell described the spring when melting snow was transformed to willow-bordered streams rushing down from the mountains, the magic of them turning into fine meadowlands the fertile soil that had been fallow for so long. Because the Indians were hostile, lately a fort had been established. From the moment I heard its name, I cherished it in my heart: Fort Independence.

To get to Inyo, a land unscarred by mines, where we might have acres of our own, became my dream—a dream John shared.

As the autumn days shortened we had our plans well made and a sufficient store of money to get them started, if only we could find horses.

Then one morning Mark came running to me. "A man has brought our horses!" he cried.

The words did not make sense, but before he was done with his excited prattle I had him by the hand and we ran to the edge of the camp, I without bonnet or shawl.

16

There, beside the big spring, were two good covered wagons, four stout horses, and a long-legged colt. A young woman sat nearby. Without even waiting for civil greeting, I asked her if the horses were for sale.

"They *were*," she said, "but a man already has bought them. If you find my husband he can tell you."

I took Mark by the hand and we hurried to the camp where the woman, whose name was Susan Cabot, said her husband had gone. I told the boy he must go to each saloon and ask for Mr. Cabot. A woman could not do it, but a man could, and he was almost a man. Poor Mark, but seven!

In the third saloon he entered, a man answered him.

"What can I do for you, son?"

I could hear Mark's voice clearly, level and filled with the importance of his mission.

"We've come to get our horses, sir."

"Your horses?" The man sounded puzzled.

"Yes, sir, our horses. The ones you brought Mother. And my colt."

"Did your mother send you to me?" the man asked.

"Of course, sir. She's waiting outside now and has the gold to pay you."

I could hear every word distinctly, and in spite of my worry, I could not help smiling at Mark's assurance.

"Then we mustn't keep your mother waiting," he chuckled. He spoke some words I could not hear, and there followed the sound of laughter in a voice that was familiar although I could not place it.

Henry Cabot came out to me, a man of our own age,

pleasant-featured. With his hat in his hand he introduced himself.

"You haven't sold the horses?" I asked quickly.

He nodded. "Sorry, but I have."

"Oh." I felt stunned. "We needed them so much. So very much."

"We'd wanted to keep going ourselves," he said gravely, "but it seemed best to stay here for a while." Then he added, "The man who bought them said they were for someone who needed them badly."

"I must see this man," I cried.

Then the saloon door opened and out came Amos Weldon. Everyone in camp regarded him as rich, although he never made any show of his wealth. I had seen him often and talked to him now and then. Always he had been particularly kind to our children.

"Mr. Weldon"—I summoned all my courage—"I have prayed for those horses. Would you let me buy them from you? I'll pay a handsome profit. . . ."

"The horses," he said, "are not for sale."

As he glared at me I could not tell whether the shrewd eyes beneath the bushy white brows were lit with anger or with laughter.

Then he took my arm, seeing how close to tears I was, and led me along the trail a little way with my Mark stalking beside me, his shoulders defiantly squared as became his mother's guardian.

"I won't *sell* the animals, Mrs. Weston," he said, when we were clear of the saloons. Then his eyes looked squarely into mine, and they were twinkling like a boy's deep in some fine mischief. "It's odd about our names," he continued, obviously marking time against something he meant to get to. "Weldon and Weston. Alike as two peas. Near enough almost to make us kinsfolk, ain't they?" Then suddenly, and a little fiercely, he blurted, "The horses are for you, ma'am. It was for you I bought them."

I opened my mouth to protest, when this Good Samaritan appeared to fly into a rage.

"Not a word out of you, ma'am! 'Tis less than I'd like to do. The matter's closed."

I offered to pay him, but the dear man would have none of that.

"One day, later, when you're all settled, perhaps," he said. "Or better, I'll come to your new home and take it out in board and lodging."

Which, indeed, was what came to pass, years later.

On that miraculous morning our talks with the Cabot family, who had owned the horses, with wonderful quickness made us feel fast friends, so that within a few days it became decided that they would cast in their fortunes with ours. No doubt my own hard picturings of what Minersville could be in winter, coupled with the little store of ready cash provided by Amos Weldon, made the quest for my valley seem attractive to them too.

My John and Henry Cabot appeared to like each other as much as did Susan and I. As for the children, from the first moment Peter Cabot saw Joan he became her cavalier. Mark did not like the arrangement and scolded at Joan; but she calmly accepted Peter's homage and completely ignored her brother. Peter told me that, aside from his

19

mother, he thought I was the prettiest lady he had ever seen.

Through my mind raced a kaleidoscope of memories of that hard journey—which was, indeed, with all its bitter experiences, no more perilous than hundreds endured by other travelers of those early days.

Once, when our fortunes were at their worst, I had come upon a cairn of rocks which marked a grave. In my diary I copied a forlorn paper found there in a rusted box:

Here lie all that is mortel of Daniel Martin Todd. He was wounded by an Injun arrer, of which wound he died. We was a party of three seeking our fortin. Now we are two left. Our companyon was a Mexican war soldier. We put our names to this dokiment telling the sukkumstances of his death lest we to perish at the hands of these savages. This is either August or September of the year 1857.

(Signed) Redman Hartfield Sloan
Jack Wilcox Brady

That day, fearing the time was close when such a record would be needed for ourselves, I prepared a paper of our own and carried it along with us, safeguarded in a stout canister.

That epitaph which we never needed was there beside me in my little room. Opening the secret compartment at

*the back of my shining rosewood desk I took out the yel-
lowed sheet. For all its forty years, having been kept so
carefully, it was still intact.*

Here perished the families of John Weston and
Henry Cabot. They consisted of John Weston,
age 30, Abigail Weston, his wife, age 25, Mark
Weston, their son, age 8, Joan Weston, their
daughter, age 5, Henry Cabot, age 30, Susan
Cabot, his wife, age 27, Peter Cabot, their son,
age 9.
They were seeking land in Inyo and perished
during the storms of September or October 1869.

*'It is rare,' I thought when I read it again as I had so
many times before, 'for one to be able to enjoy one's own
epitaph so long after it was written!'*

*Then I replaced the precious document. With the desk
compartment open I laid my hand for a moment upon a
sealed envelope that lay there, an envelope that only I
knew existed. My mind went back to the time that envelope was given me, eleven years after we had come to
Golden Valley.*

When Amos Weldon finally came to visit his "name-
sakes," as he had threatened to do that day his gift of the
horses helped so much our own departure from Minersville, the years had made him a truly old man, his hair and
beard snow-white, his frame gaunt, although the keen blue

21

eyes beneath the bushy brows remained young and forever twinkling. All he said of his own affairs was that he had sold his mines. He seemed very happy with us, but at the end of a fortnight he announced quite briskly he would be leaving, although I told him there was no reason for him to go then, or ever.

"Now that warms the cockles of a man's heart," he exclaimed, his face lighting up. "But you've a pretty full house, and—"

"We're saving to build a large one," I interrupted. "And it won't be long before we can."

He looked hard at me for a moment, then nodded absently and walked away. A little later I saw him talking to John who was irrigating his trees, and when he came back to the house his face was like a thundercloud. Stalking straight to his room, I behind him to learn what the trouble was, he began throwing things into his carpetbags. I walked in and asked him point-blank what was wrong.

The old man straightened up and glared at me. "What's wrong? Everything! I offer to give your fool husband money to build a new house, and he puts me in my place. That's what he does."

For a moment I could only stare. Then I burst out laughing and laughed until tears came. Such a tempest in a teapot! All the poor lamb had tried to do was to help us, and stiff-necked John had been properly insulted, and doubtless insulted him. Presently he began to laugh too, and in a few minutes we were clinging to one another, too weak too stand. Then, when we had recovered, we wiped our eyes and sought out John. It did not take long to mend matters there, for I could see that John already felt contrite, and I left the two talking together. Presently Mr. Weldon came to me and took firm hold of my arm.

"I want to talk to you seriously," he said. "Having your own family and neighbors, Abigail, you can't know what it's like to be old and lonely even if you happen to be rich."

He looked for a time at the mountains, keeping hold of my hand.

"But it's the things gold can't buy that I want, Abigail. Look." He jerked a thumb toward the window. David was playing in the yard. "The love of a lad like him. Joan's sweetness. Peter and Mark comin' to me with their little troubles. Some of 'em you don't even guess, close to 'em as you are."

"Well," I said, trying to keep my voice casual until he had time to recover his composure, "if that's all you want, the thing is settled. You'll just stay and put up with inconveniences until such time as we can build our new house."

"Stay I'm going to," he retorted. "But I'm not putting up with no inconveniences. You're buildin' that house now." He poked a long finger into my ribs, just as was his wont with the boys. "You're buildin' that house with a room in it for me. John said so. He did. I'm your Uncle Amos recently come from the East, by doggie. And John said that, too, he did."

"Why, so you are!" I cried. "My, but it's good to see you. Welcome home, Uncle Amos."

It was the end of the summer in which we lost our own boy David, who had been so very dear to the old man, that Uncle Amos one day came to me.

"There's something I want you to do for me, Abigail," he said, and I realized unhappily how old his eyes had grown. "Take this." He thrust a heavy manila envelope into my hands. "You've the best sense of them all."

He paused and stared broodingly at me. "You're a good woman, Abigail," he went on presently. "And a smart one." A faint smile twisted the corners of his mouth. "Although not so smart or good as you might be! But there's one thing sure. You're to be trusted."

He tapped the envelope and his old eyes were keen again. "In there is twenty-five thousand dollars, Abigail. Gold, my dear. There's a paper from the San Francisco Mint says the gold is lyin' there, waitin'!"

I think I must have gasped, for he waved an impatient hand.

"I sold the mines for fifty thousand and had a bit put away on top of that, didn't I?" he demanded. "Did you think I'd spent it all?" He glared at me.

I had not thought at all and was too taken aback to answer. Here was romancing of a sort more incredible than one was apt to read about in those novels John had teased me about. After all, ours was an incredible land. Certainly I knew that in Amos Weldon's way of thinking it was altogether reasonable to give what he wished to whom he wished, and in whatever way suited his fancy.

When the old man began to speak again, he appeared to be selecting his words with care as though he had

24

thought out long before exactly what he wanted to say. "It's gold I'm turnin' over to you, Abigail. Clean gold from out the earth. No one cheated to get it." He wagged an old finger at me. "It's the cleanest money there is, that kind."

He paused again and it was as though I could see him thinking.

"You keep it safe. Don't spend it except for something very special." He patted my hand. "Somethin' very special," he repeated. "If you needed it now you could have it, but you don't. Right now you've got everythin'. But you never can tell." He wagged his old head sagely. "Things come about that the wisest can't foresee. And that's what this gold is for." He tapped the envelope again.

"So that's done," he went on briskly. "I'm gettin' old and tired. 'Twon't be long now until I'm joinin' Davie. Sssh! Sssh! A man can't live forever, and wouldn't want to. And one more thing. Tell no one at all you have it. That's positive. Not even John. Come the time to use it you'll know well enough."

For the next three or four days the old man seemed curiously contented. On a Tuesday he had Little John drive him over the ranch, stopping for a visit both at Mark's and the Cabot's. He seemed a little tired that night but in good spirits, although when bedtime came and he said goodnight his voice was wistful. John helped him upstairs and sat with him for a time.

In the morning, when Gim Lee took up his coffee, Uncle Amos had gone to join David.

25

With my backward-looking thoughts caught up, the precious envelope from Uncle Amos lay beside me, a bridge of sorts between that night and the long ago. Tenderly then I replaced it in the desk, closed the little hidden drawer and with a last look at the shadowed Sierra, went back to my room and to John.

Chapter 3.

WHATEVER prompted me—perhaps my spate of memories was responsible, for it left me oddly disturbed—as John climbed into the buckboard on his way to town next morning, I asked him not to say anything about Abby's young man, or of the government's being already at work on George's Creek.

"For heaven's sake! Why not?" he said impatiently. "It's no secret."

"No-o. I suppose not. Still, I wish you wouldn't. Not till after Saturday, anyway."

"What's got into you?" he demanded. "There are a lot of people interested in this thing. Why should they have to wait till Abby's fetched this young fellow in and showed him off to us?"

"Well, I don't remember that he actually said he was working for the government," I admitted, uncertainly.

John picked up the reins.

"That's easy enough to settle," he said. "I'll just hunt

him up and find out first-hand. Ought to do that anyhow, I guess. There wouldn't be any other engineers around," he added, reasonably.

Not understanding my own reluctance, I clutched at his arm. "Please don't, John," I begged. "Don't do that. Let Abby have her little triumph. It means so much to a girl. It's only a few days."

He laid down the reins again and his face darkened.

"Do you really mean that I'm not to mention this young fellow, or the government being here, or even to go look him up myself? Are you standing there and seriously telling me that?"

I nodded, unhappily.

John grunted and picked up the reins. Without a good-bye or even another glance at me, he clucked to the team and was off down the drive. I was still standing there when Abby rode up.

"What's the matter, Hanny?" she exclaimed. "You look as though someone had bitten you."

"Your grandfather's angry," I said.

"Well, don't look so forlorn. He'll get over it." She checked her ready laugh and slipped her arm about me. "What is it?"

I felt more foolish than ever, trying to explain my behavior to my granddaughter.

"I don't know what got into me, but I asked him not to tell about your friend, Mr. Allen. At least until after Saturday. He was all for going right to see him, now."

"And you wouldn't let him?"

"No. That's why he's cross."

"Well, you did exactly right." She nodded vigorously.

"It—it seemed that way to me, too," I faltered. She tethered her horse and went into the house with her hand on my shoulder. "Why would it spoil things, Abby?" I asked, wondering if she could find words for my stubborn inward feeling that puzzled even me.

"I don't know." She shook her head. "Truly, I don't. But it would. After Saturday, I don't care."

We went into the sitting room, and Abby drummed her fingers lightly on the top of the sofa where we sat. She sent me a sudden, thoughtful look.

"Tell me, Hanny darling, when you first met Grandpa John, did you feel like something was gone inside you, here?" She laid her hand on her stomach. There was a sort of pathos in the gesture. My thoughts flew back with incredible ease to that first meeting between John and me. I recalled vividly the trembling, the wordlessness when there was such a need for words—any words to tide me over the moment whose bigness I could not understand.

"Yes, Abby," I said, bringing my eyes and mind back to her.

In the clear morning light, her face looked small and intense, her wide eyes faintly shadowed as though she had not slept enough in the night.

She nodded, solemnly. "That's how I felt yesterday— and still do. I don't suppose it matters one bit who sees him and when." Her voice rose to an anxious note. "Every- thing is perfectly all right. I know that. Yet I have the most horrible fear that some little thing, something nobody's thought about, might come up before David's had a chance

29

to see the family and the family to see him. And I want us to . . . to like him for himself, not because he happens to be an engineer working for the government. Am I too silly for anything, Hanny?"

I took her hand. "If you're silly, child, I'm doubly so. Nothing is going to spoil anything." I wanted so much to make them true that my words had a grimness I had not intended to give them.

Abby's great day came at last, though there were times when I wondered, with her, if it ever would. Until that mad week, I had always thought the house clean, meals bountiful, and, thanks to Gim Lee's artistry, well cooked, and the yard and garden neat and colorful. Altogether, the attractions of our home seemed very real.

Abby, who had always avoided anything approaching a domestic duty, suddenly took complete charge of our establishment. She changed the furniture about. Rugs were dragged out and beaten, windows, mirrors, and pictures washed till they glittered. Mary, our house girl, relapsed into stolid Indian sullenness. There were bouts with Gim Lee that sent Abby from the kitchen with a stormy face and muttered threats. Joe Ramirez, the gardener, wailed with eyes raised to the dazzling blue sky, "Am I God that I should keep the leaves from falling?"

"I do wish Dad and Uncle Mark and Little John could be here," Abby sighed, during one of her breathing spells. In this summer season, the boys were up in Monache with the cattle. "Still," she brightened, "maybe it's just as well. Uncle Mark would ask ten thousand questions. Dad wouldn't say anything except, 'Please pass the pickles,' or, 'Plenty, thank you.' Little John wouldn't utter a syllable. Much as I love the Injun, there are times when he gives me the creeps!" She tossed a lock of hair off her forehead. "No, I guess it's better to stake-break David sort of gentle. Let him take a few of us at a time. We're a sort of overwhelming family, Hanny, come to consider." Her eyes, gravely dark, studied the pattern of the rug.

John had not held against me our little misunderstanding about David Allen. Henry grumbled some, but mildly. Joan was curious, as any mother would be, and a little hurt that Abby had not confided very much in her.

"Is he a nice young fellow, Mother?" she asked me, anxiously. "I can't get a thing out of Abby except, 'Wait and see.'"

"He's better than 'nice,' Joanie," I consoled her. "You'll like him as much as I did."

John showed more impatience than any of us for Saturday to come, but for different reasons.

"I want to find out what this chap's up to," he said bluntly. "That is"—his manner became almost mincing, his brows lifted—"if you and Abby approve."

On Saturday afternoon Abby arrived in her buggy, a huge valise thrown in the back. Her eyes were shining. She demanded breathlessly the moment she was in the door, "Everything's going to be all right . . . for certain, isn't it?"

"Of course," I laughed. "Hasn't Gim Lee, poor thing, been up since daybreak? Hasn't he run me out of my own kitchen a dozen times?" I thought it more politic not to repeat the chief scene that had taken place that morning.

Gim Lee had come to me, his moon face set in yellow immobility. "You tellee Abbee lee me lone," he had ordered belligerently.

"What's the matter, Gim Lee?" I had asked gently.

"Whassa malla?" he shrilled. "Evlythin' malla! Abbee say make em consoom soup. Bellywash! *Me* say mushloom soup. She get mad. I get mad. Maybe I quit."

"No, Gim Lee." I had patted him on the back, gently. "You wouldn't go back on Abby today. Make any kind of soup you want."

"All light. All light. Make em mushloom soup." He had trotted back into the kitchen.

When I told John about it, he had chortled, "I guess we get mushroom soup."

Abby had not been in the kitchen five minutes after her arrival that afternoon before a tumult of vocal combat exploded. Gim Lee was shrilling, Abby trying without success to keep her voice firm and dignified and low-pitched. "Mushloom soup" swirled and eddied about "consomme" and explosive shrieks of "You get outa here" from Gim Lee. I fled to the dining room so as to be out of sight but within call.

The curtains were drawn, the room in half light. The table was beautifully prepared. Gim Lee had been at the task of setting it, off and on, since early morning. Every piece of silver, every glass was polished, twinkling from their places on the beautiful Irish linen cloth. Gim Lee's boxes of red geraniums sent their faintly astringent perfume into the room. On the sideboard stood a silver bowl of roses

I had cut that morning. But something was missing—my cranberry-glass bowl for a centerpiece. There would be no strawberries for it at this time of year, but our early Manzanar red apples would do as well.

I slipped out the back way to the cool room and brought a basket of the apples. I was just polishing the last one when Abby burst in, her face flushed.

"I could kill that heathen Chinee," she raged. "He's spoiled everything with his pig-headedness."

"As he's spoiled everything in here, for example?" I suggested, holding my head on one side to look at the apples in the glass bowl.

Abby's eyes ranged the table, moved to the sideboard, the window-boxes, the speckless carpet, and came remorsefully to my face. She drew a long breath. "I guess I'll have to forgive him his mushloom soup," she muttered. "And you, Hanny darling, you've set out your precious cranberry-glass bowl." She put her fingers out and stroked its sides lovingly. "How beautiful it is! How beautiful everything is! Bless Gim Lee's old heathen heart."

That day some duties had kept John on the ranch. Before he had even started to change from his blue jeans, Abby tapped on our door and then stood before us.

She wore a gown of cornflower blue, and her hair was up, giving a hint of thinness to the childlike contours of her face. Her eyes looked larger for the faint blue shadows beneath them. With appalling suddenness this beloved grandchild had become a woman, and the knowledge filled my heart with a mixture of uneasiness and adoration.

"Do I look all right?" she asked, preening and turning

33

and holding her head on one side as her mother had done when she was Abby's age.

"Lovely, Abby, my darling," I assured her.

John looked her over in silence, pulled his lip, and frowned at the shining coronet of her hair.

"I guess you'll have to do," he said dourly. I saw a sudden flare of his nostrils, a proud lighting of the eyes I knew so well. I slipped to his side and felt for his hand. His fingers closed tight about mine, and he added huskily, "You look very beautiful, my dear—only too grown up."

Abby's laughter stopped short in sudden concern, and her eyes darted over John. "You'd better be getting dressed yourself, Grandpa," she warned. "There's no time to kill."

"Dressed?" John echoed blankly. "What's the matter with these?" He looked down stupidly at his jeans. "They're clean enough."

Abby clutched her head in both her hands despairingly. "Grandpa! Doesn't it even *begin* to penetrate a little, little bit that tonight isn't just an ordinary occasion?"

John laughingly pulled Abby to him for a hasty kiss.

"All right, all right. Don't shoot. I'll slick up like any city dude! And I'm going to have a lot of questions to pop to that young fellow, too."

Most of the young men I had known would have appeared ill at ease thrust into the midst of a strange family. But David Allen somehow was quite at home with us from the very first.

When Abby opened the door to his knock, his eyes widened and he gave her a special quick smile. Then he

34

was acknowledging introductions, and promptly he and John and Henry were talking together, with Abby hovering near to avert any cross-examination she disapproved.

I kept a sharp eye on the dining-room doors. I had told Gim Lee to give us half an hour after our guest arrived before announcing dinner, and Abby had painstakingly instructed him as to how that ceremony should be performed. He was to open the door quietly, step into the room, and say simply, "Dinner is served." He had taken it so blandly that I wondered exactly what would happen.

I saw the door open a crack and a round yellow face thrust into the opening. A sing-song voice chanted, "Glub ledee. Come catchee. Me throw 'em out."

I bit my lip as I looked at Abby. But she hadn't even heard.

When we had all taken our places, Gim Lee shuffled in with a bowl of mushroom soup which he set before David. He always served me first, whether at company or family gatherings, and I knew this was a deliberate departure.

"Mushloom soup," he cackled. He beamed at Abby. "Abbee she say consoom. Me say mushloom. This mushloom." He poked a yellow finger at the edge of the bowl. "Stick to lib likee hellee. You betcha."

Poor Abby looked embarrassed enough to leave the table. John lifted his napkin to his lips but couldn't hide his laughing eyes. Joan threw me a startled and chagrined look, and I could cheerfully have boxed Gim Lee's celestial ears. Only David seemed completely unperturbed. He grinned at Gim Lee as if they were old cronies.

35

"It does stick to the ribs," he agreed roundly. "And don't let Miss Abby run over you."

As easily as that, David Allen gained an undying friend, and Gim Lee radiated triumph as he proceeded to serve the rest of us. Abby looked angry, then uncertain, then she giggled; and all of us laughed outright, banishing the awkward moment.

"It's just as well you like mushroom soup—if you do," John explained. "You see now who's boss around here."

As he vanished into the kitchen to lord it over Indian Mary, with an oriental grin Gim Lee cast a parting sentence over his shoulder: "This man smart, you betcha. Allee same Little John."

David Allen, with the smile still on his face turned to Abby. "Just what might that mean?"

"The highest of compliments."

"And who would Little John be?"

"Little John," she explained, "is an Indian. A full-blood Indian." Then she added demurely, "He's my uncle."

That brought David's eyebrows up.

"You see," she went on gravely, "he's Hanny's son."

"*Wait* a minute!"

Then Abby, before either John or I could set things straight, her eyes laughing and her voice gay, told our guest how the Indian baby, son of the renegade Joaquin Jim, had been taken into our family and grown up as one of us.

"You see, primitive people like us are always taking in the queerest characters!"

"Such as surveyors, eh?" he teased.

36

"Oh, Little John is in a class by himself," Abby assured him. "I only hope you get along as well with him as you do with your new friend Gim Lee. But it will take you about a year to know whether you're going to be loved or scalped, because Little John never says a word. But he sees everything and hears everything and knows everything. He's a sort of outdoor version of this Sherlock Holmes we're reading about, flavored with a dash of coyote cunning plus an eagle's eyesight and the gift of a fox to read signs and follow trails."

"Evidently quite a person, this uncle of yours!" David replied. "Miss Abby, if I stay in this country I hope I'll always be on the same side as your fabulous Little John."

"I hope so," she said gravely.

After a third helping of Gim Lee's famous fried chicken, David looked at me with a smile.

"You're spoiling me, Mrs. Weston," he said. "We don't get quite this sort of food in camp."

John had been waiting for some opening. "It's a fine profession you follow, Mr. Allen," he said genially. "We think a good deal of you engineers in these parts."

"That's good of you, sir," David Allen returned politely. "I like the work. Wanted to do it ever since I can remember." The pleasant smile left his face and a shadow touched it. "It was my father's work, too. He's dead, now."

"I'm sorry to hear that."

There was brief silence; then John added, "I suppose we'll be seeing a lot of you surveyors around from now on?"

"Yes, sir, I expect so. You've lived in this valley a long time?"

"Practically since the first white man," Abby put in eagerly. "Hanny and Grandpa John and Grampy"—she nodded toward Henry—"and Dad and Mother and Uncle Mark all came overland forty years ago. Some day Hanny must tell you all about their trip. Why, they built Manzanar!"

"With a little help here and there," John put in.

But Abby wasn't to be stopped now. Her pride in us had the ascendancy and she ran on excitedly, "You four started everything. If it hadn't been for you. . . . Hanny, tell David about the time you mixed the dirt with the water and put it in your brooch."

With Abby's starry eyes demanding it, her bright head tipped forward a little, I had no choice but to go through the old story again.

"That was a long time ago." I found myself talking to David Allen as if only we two were there. "It was in March, 1870. John—that's my husband, your host"—I smiled at John whom I could see just then as he had looked forty years before—"had just plowed the first furrow in our first field. I don't believe people today with their lands all tamed around them can quite understand the thrill of that. . . ." For the moment my voice tapered off, taut with emotion.

In the little silence David said quietly, "I believe we can, ma'am."

"Henry—that's Abby's grandfather—set the plow and with John driving the team the plowshare bit deep into the rich soil that had been there untouched since the beginning. My breath held so still as I watched that first
38

furrow curl its dark sides upward to the sun that I almost suffocated. It was true and straight. I cried a little."

They were all very still.

"Oh, Hanny!" The marvel of love was in Abby's voice as she leaned across to lay her hand on mine.

"You see, I'd waited so long for that day. That morning our dreams at last were coming true."

"And then?" Gently Abby urged me to the end of the little story.

"Later, I slipped out of the house and went back to the new-plowed land. Visions. . . ." I tried to smile through the tears that foolishly clouded my eyes. "Visions clutched my heart. In my mind, as I stood there, the long brown land that was our valley became transformed into a carpet of green. Fat cattle grazed the meadows, and colts frolicked knee-deep in grass. I saw tall poplars marking the borders of our ranch, cottonwoods giving their shade to a friendly home. Those things, you know, actually have happened in the happy years since that morning. So then I took a bit of the soft earth and put it in my brooch, earth from the first plowing of our first field. That little fragment of our good earth, sweet with the water of our streams, ever since I have kept here."

I laid my hand on the old brooch hanging as it often did about my neck. Worn thin as it was, I loved it better than any jewelry. The cherished treasure that it held was an open sesame to the youth my husband and I had left behind us.

When I was through, John, bless him, got up and came behind me, laying a little kiss at the nape of my neck.

"Good girl," he whispered.

"That was pretty fine," David said seriously. "I never heard the like before."

Then Abby was bubbling again. "Oh, that's just one of a hundred tales Hanny could tell!" she assured our guest gaily. "But even with its history counted out, don't you love our valley?"

"You bet." I had a notion there were other words on the tip of David's tongue, but he finished discreetly, "What I've seen of it."

She had the grace to blush becomingly at the emphasis he gave the words.

I asked our guest, then, if he knew what the name of our mountains meant.

"Inyo? No. Please tell me."

At my nod Abby, all eagerness to display her wisdom, explained that the word was from the language of the Shoshone Indians and meant the "Land of Lost Borders."

"And Owens Lake," she continued, "was named for Dick Owen in 1845 by Fremont, who tagged about everything else that wasn't already labeled. Dick," she added sagely, "was a pal of Kit Carson's and quite a lad himself."

"Our granddaughter," John observed, "is Golden Valley's fairest font of knowledge."

David nodded gravely. "A true native daughter, sir."

"But just you wait till you get up on Top," Abby rattled on. "Wait til you see Monache. Thousands of acres of meadows green as emeralds, too beautiful to be true. I *hope* I'm there the first time you watch the deer come drifting out from the timber at dusk."

40

"I hope so, too," David said at once, relieving me a little, for Abby's runaway enthusiasm had made me uneasy. I didn't want the young man to think she had begun to arrange things for him. He gave a short laugh. "But I'm afraid the city didn't hire me to go ranging through the high mountains with beautiful ladies—and that's my bad luck!"

"City?" John echoed. "What city?"

"Why, Los Angeles, sir."

Chapter 4.

SUDDEN tension pervaded the room. A coldness settled round my heart. I felt Abby stiffen beside me. Henry sat bolt upright as though a sharp point had prodded him. John laid down his fork and stared at David Allen.

"Aren't you a government engineer, then?" he asked, and his words were like little stones dropping into a well.

"No, sir. I work for Los Angeles. The Water Department, sir."

"I don't understand." Perplexity drew sudden lines in John's face. "What possible interest can Los Angeles have up this way?"

"Water, sir," young Allen replied promptly.

"Water? Up here? What for?"

"To get an adequate supply. Los Angeles is growing fast, you know, and the talk is that it's coming to the end of its row for water."

42

"But in California you can't rob one watershed to feed another," Henry objected bluntly.

David Allen's direct look passed from John's troubled face to Henry's faintly belligerent one.

"If you say so, sir. I don't know. I suppose there are laws covering that."

"There are," John answered grimly. "How does Los Angeles plan to get this water?"

"Why, buy it, I suppose." David began to look a little embarrassed and a little anxious. His eyes sought Abby's through the puzzlement of the sharp attention that suddenly focused on him. There was a dusky flush on his cheekbones, and I had the uncomfortable feeling that as a hostess I was somehow failing him. But I could not stop this conversation. Too much seemed to be at stake, too much to be clarified. . . . "All I know," David went on, "is that a good many of us have been sent up here—my crew is only one of them—to take water measurements, tables, run contour lines, and make general preliminary surveys. After that's done, I don't know what happens." He shook his head. "I hadn't really looked that far."

The room was very still. A miller moth beat futilely at the window screen. The little sounds of the night outside penetrated the stillness. I felt a blind groping in my lap. It was Abby's hand, moist and cold, hunting mine. John was frowning down the table, playing with a spoon. He drew a long breath.

"I'm afraid you startled us badly, Mr. Allen," he said, and I knew he was having a struggle to keep his voice casual. "You see, we've a reclamation project of our own

43

just under way. It's a long story that I won't bother you with now, but I think you can imagine what a shock it is to find Los Angeles up here after the same water we're expecting to use."

"Yes, sir, I can. And I've never heard a breath of your reclamation district," David said, earnestly. He was not looking at Abby now, and I pressed her cold fingers.

John forced a smile.

"Well," he said, "take my word for it. We have one. A pretty husky one at that. Ever hear of a man named Enderby?"

"By reputation only, sir. James Enderby. Consulting engineer, and good as they come, I've heard."

"I'm glad of that," John said dryly. "He's chief engineer of the project."

David Allen frowned thoughtfully. "That's funny," he said. "Our boys up Bishop way report to him. Doesn't make sense after what you've just told me, does it?"

"What's that?" John sat up so straight I thought he was going to leap from his chair. He leaned forward, and the water trembled in his glass. "Los Angeles men report to Enderby? Why, it's not believable!"

"Yes, sir. I agree with you that it's pretty hard to believe. But I'm not mistaken."

John marked a few intricate patterns on the tablecloth with his spoon.

"I don't want to urge you to betray any confidence, Mr. Allen," he said slowly. "But if there is any way—any more you can feel it right to tell us about this thing, we'll

44

be very grateful. It's new to us, as you can see; a bolt right out of the blue."

"I'm afraid I actually know mighty little that's authentic. Of course, there's talk among the boys. The city plans an aqueduct from here down to San Fernando, about one hundred miles. Spending thirty million dollars. Hydro-electric power will be developed. But that's all talk. I wouldn't vouch for a word of it. Hadn't concerned myself with it."

John seemed to pull himself together, smiling apologetically at his guest. He thanked him for his candor, apologized for the cross-examination, and cast about for a change of subject. I tapped the bell for Gim Lee, and he popped into the room so suddenly that I was certain he had been crouching with his ear to the keyhole.

As soon as David Allen had gone, John demanded, "Did that young fellow *claim* to be a government man?"

"He did not," Abby answered defiantly. "All he said was that he had a surveying crew up the creek. We jumped to conclusions." Her voice had a little break in it.

"That's all I wanted to know," John said. "That lets him out."

"It doesn't let his bosses out!" Henry protested. "Mark my words, John Weston. It's the beginning of a colossal steal."

"Well, if it is, David Allen hasn't any part in it," Abby blazed. "Can't you see that? You heard what he. . . ."

"Just a minute, everybody," John said, holding up a warning hand. "You're right, Abby. Young Allen has nothing to do with it. He's just a decent young fellow hired on

45

a job. As far as its being a steal is concerned, Henry, we don't know what it is—yet. Let's wait till we find out."

"Wait?" Henry snorted.

"We'll start on the trail first thing in the morning," John went on. "First, we'll see Frank Masters. Then we'll go up to Bishop and smoke out this Enderby business. When we know what we're up against we'll figure what to do next. Right?"

"You'll find yourself up against plenty," Henry prophesied gloomily. "Los Angeles doesn't do things halfway. Look how they jumped twenty-five miles to tidewater to get themselves a harbor. Then they get laws passed to give themselves terminal rates. They play for keeps."

"They do," John answered patiently. "All I want are some facts to go on. What we've got now is the story of a young fellow who admits he doesn't know anything for sure except that he's hired by Los Angeles to do surveying up here. All the rest of what he told. . . ."

"He told you all he knew!" Abby cried. "He answered every single question you asked him."

John looked at her somberly.

"I'm sure of that, Abby. There's no occasion for you to fly to his defense. He doesn't need it. If it goes anywhere at all, it goes a lot deeper than young Allen."

"But neither Los Angeles nor anybody else can come here and take our water," I said vehemently.

John's eyes met mine with a hardness I had seen in them at bad times, before.

"That's right," he said so quietly that a little shiver ran down my back. "But they can buy it."

46

There was little talk between John and me as we prepared for bed. He had settled comfortably on his pillow and closed his eyes before I was half undressed. Suddenly he called my name in a sleepy voice.

"Guess there's something to this woman's intuition nonsense," he grunted. "Just as well you didn't let me spill the beans that day I was rarin' to, Abbie girl."

I fumbled at a button, my hand trembling. What petty triumph there might have been in having John call me right was lost in my towering distress, a distress inextricably mixed with my personal love for my granddaughter and my wider concern for this valley into which we had thrust our deepest roots.

As I moved into my little room above the verandah for a few moments of quiet thinking, I heard a soft rustling, and Abby stood beside me in her coral-colored dressing gown. Above it, the untanned portion of her throat had a fragile look, her eyes seemed too large in their shadows. All my years of motherhood seemed to concentrate in a single pain beneath my breast as I saw how white and troubled was the face she raised to me. She had always been so gay, so untouched by gravity.

"I knew I'd find you here," she said. "In your thinking room." She tried to smile as she leaned against the sill, staring out into the night.

"There's plenty to think about, I'm afraid," I said quietly.

As we sat together, myriad nocturnal sounds throbbed through the darkness. The croaking of frogs beside the water ditches; the wind in the cottonwood branches brushing the roof; the crickets' song; the sudden mournful bellow of a steer in the meadow; the nicker of a horse. A band of coyotes broke into their eerie song. Against the sky loomed the darker, broken wall of the High Sierra, immutable and calm. Close at hand, as always, was the rustle of the leaves of our beloved trees.

"It *can* be pretty bad, can't it, Hanny?" The voice from the window sounded faint and small.

I pretended a calmness I did not feel. "We don't know, child."

"It could make all the difference between David and me."

"Not unless you let it, Abby," I said staunchly. "He isn't responsible."

"He works for Los Angeles. . . ."

"So do a good many other fine young men, I expect."

"You heard what Grampy had to say. Los Angeles will be against everything we're for."

"We don't know that. Even so. . . ."

She made an impatient gesture.

"Oh, yes, we do, Hanny dear. We knew it the moment David told us whom he represents. We knew it in the sitting room after he'd gone." She drew a caught breath. "He wouldn't have left so early if things hadn't been like this. We'll be on one side, David on the other. We know it and he knows it."

I wanted to go to her and take her in my arms. Once, long ago, she had fallen and cut her knee. Then, as now, she had not cried, but had looked at me, white-faced and large-eyed. I had bound her wound and held her close. But now a curious reluctance prevented my touching her.

Here was a deep wound I could not bandage. I stood dumbly, watching her straight young back and the uncurving set of her slim shoulders.

And when John was back from Bishop, it became clear that the wound was not alone for this girl so suddenly in love. It was a dreadful threat to all of us and to the very existence of the valley that was our life.

John told me the story of his trip as precisely as he could, pacing restlessly about the room, flinging himself down into a chair, then moving about again. I tried not to let his nervousness become contagious, and followed as closely as I could.

"Frank Masters wasn't much impressed to start with," he said. "He'd heard Los Angeles had been nosing round. He didn't think that meant anything. Said they're notorious for that. Anyhow, with the government stepping in, whatever L.A. might have in mind's a dead horse."

John said he hadn't wasted time arguing with Frank. "Henry and I went on to Bishop to see Will Fiske and persuaded Frank to follow us. He didn't want to much." John looked moodily out at his poplars grown tall and proud over the years. Behind them the mountains danced in the heat waves.

"I pushed the team faster than I wanted, but even then Will was getting ready to go to bed by the time we got there. Had his shirt off and suspenders hanging down when we crowded in on him."

My imagination pictured the yellow lamplight streaming out the open door upon John and Henry in their travel-stained linen dusters. I could see Will, roly-poly little brownie-like man that he was, a bundle of brains behind a guileless face, who'd been our lawyer and our friend for years.

"He was pretty startled to see us at that time of night. A lot more so when I got through telling him what brought us. But like Frank, he was inclined to consider the whole thing moonshine."

The three had argued for a time, then John asked Will point-blank what he knew about Enderby. Will had said at once that he was all right, an A-1 engineer. Then, John said, Will had squinted up his eyes and thought for a moment and said Enderby wasn't exactly the sort of fellow one would go fishing with.

"I kept digging," John told me. "I knew that boy wasn't just gossiping the other night, Abbie. He's all right, that young Allen. I knew there was something wrong somewhere, and there was bound to be a loose clew if we could get on to it that would lead us to the hitch.

"So I took a new tack. Being after water, they'd naturally file on any that was free and buy up any water-owning land they could. I asked Will if there had been any unusual activity in land transfers lately.

"That made him sit up! He squawked right out, 'Jee-rusalem—and I never gave it a minute's thought! Put 'em down to natural speculation, account of the district.'

"I asked if he meant sales, and he said, 'No—options.' Thought back and said he bet he'd notarized twenty in the past month. He was squirming into his shirt and pretty near ran us the couple of blocks to his office."

John took one of his turns about the room and I pressed my hands together in my lap and managed to sit still, though I wanted to pace with him. I knew Will's office. Dingy and dusty with books and papers scattered in every possible space.

"It was hot as a bake oven in there," John said. "And smelly. You know—dust, old tobacco smoke, musty books, moldy old carpet. The water kept dripping out of the tap over the sink and it seemed to make the heat worse than ever." John pressed his lips together, swung about, and looked at me as a thought occurred to him. "Funny," he said, "come to think of it, dripping water ought to sound cool. That didn't.

"It took us over an hour, but we ran it down. Will's notary records showed about fifteen thousand acres optioned around Bishop and another ten thousand between there and Big Pine. A few names were scattered in the lot, but most of it went to a George W. Bushnell. The name of Los Angeles wasn't anywhere."

I felt that I should make some comment, but had no words worth saying. My interest was like a pain pressing against me and holding me silent. For the first time in many years I had the feeling that our security, my world itself, was falling apart. . . . I pinned my mind to what John was saying.

"As fast as Will dug the items out of his records, Henry jotted them down and I marked them off the map. We'd just finished when Frank walked in. He looked hot and cranky. He laid his Stetson down in the cleanest place he could find on Will's desk—you know how particular

Frank is about his hat, Abbie—and said, 'You boys laid your ghosts now?'

"I told him not so's he could notice it. 'Come here,' I said, 'I want to show you something.'

"I was standing at that big map of Bishop Will's got hanging in his office. 'See those?' I said, and I ticked off the optioned ranches fast as I could. I'd circled each one of 'em in red.

"Frank studied them for a minute. 'All right,' he snapped. 'What about it? What do those red circles mean?'

"I told him they meant that every one of those ranches had been optioned out in the past month.

"'Who to?' Frank says, and I told him different people, but mostly to a fellow named Bushnell. 'George W. Bushnell,' I said.

"Frank wanted to know who he was, and I couldn't tell him, but Will explained that Bushnell was a newcomer, little nondescript chap with one of those hearing devices on his ear. Will said he hung around the saloons a lot but wasn't one to treat often. Not friendly, either. Frank just grunted and went back to studying the map. When he spoke up he sounded scared.

"'I got a lot of money strewed around here,' he said. 'You think this might tie up with that Los Angeles business?' I said I didn't know but it didn't look good. Frank said it looked like hell to him, and he spread his big paw over the map. 'I got a lot of money strewed around there,' he said again.

"There didn't seem to be much to say to that. Frank did have money loaned out on pretty near every ranch I'd circled and a lot more besides. Bishop ranches have always been good risks.

"Will told Frank not to let it bother him. Sold or not, Will said, those ranches were all good for Frank's loans. Frank turned on him like a trapped bearcat. 'Hell,' he snarled. 'It ain't them I'm worrying about. It's these here.' He wiped his hand right over the whole district. 'The best ranches here never owned a drop o' water in their history. Been living off of seepage for fifty years. Take that seepage away and where'll they be?'

"Somehow or other, none of us had thought about that. It didn't make the picture a bit prettier, Abbie, you can see that. Henry was popeyed. He started to sputtering that they couldn't do that—you know how Henry gets all riled up. 'Maybe they can't,' Frank said, dry as you please, 'but they'd bust a hamstring trying.'"

John flung himself wearily onto the sofa and rubbed his hands across his face. "That's what they'll do, too," he said, "and it'll mean ruin, Abigail. Half Golden Valley does live off of seepage water. Take it away and the desert will have the land back again inside of three years! If you doubt me, look at any abandoned homestead."

"But, John," I cried, "they wouldn't—they couldn't do that. . . ." I thought of Henry's ranch, Tom Ellison's, the Schultzes', every one of them fertile from seepage water.

I could hear the clock ticking in the hall as we sat silently, stricken by the enormity of the threat that hung over us and all our community. When I could bear my

53

thoughts no longer, I huskily urged John to go on with his story.

"I told the boys everything that young Allen told us, especially about city men reporting to Enderby. Will wouldn't believe it, but the rest of us were ready to swallow anything by then. Poor Frank had turned gray around the gills and looked sick. He had to hang onto a chair not to wobble on his pins. He called Enderby a name I won't favor you with and said we were talking to him first thing in the morning."

John shifted his position, leaned forward, and drummed his fingers nervously on his knee.

"We did talk to Enderby. He's a tough customer. Hard as a barrel of nails. Coldest eyes I ever saw. His office is an old storeroom, but he's got it hung full of blueprints. He had a drafting table at the back and two men working at it. Enderby didn't so much as get up when we came in. Nodded to Will and Frank, and got out a 'pleased to meet you' when Will introduced Henry and me. He didn't sound pleased, and if he said anything civil such as 'have a chair,' I didn't hear it.

"I didn't waste any time. I told him what we'd heard and found, not mentioning any names. He never batted an eye, just pulled away on a dead pipe. When I got through he said, 'I know all about that.' Imagine how I felt, how we all felt, getting an answer like that from a man supposed to be in charge of our district! When I cooled off a little, I told him in that case I assumed steps were being taken to checkmate L.A.

"'Not that I know of,' he said, looking me straight in

the eye and not even bothering to take the pipe out of his mouth.

"That's when I did lose my temper. I asked him if he realized what this L.A. grab would mean, what he thought of his responsibilities as chief engineer of our district. I got an answer all right, but not the kind I was expecting."

John looked angrily about the pleasant sitting room. Then he sighed and pushed his hair off his forehead and went on.

"Enderby said flatly that he didn't know what I was talking about. That he wasn't chief engineer of anything. As far as he knew we didn't have a reclamation district. That was too much for Frank. He was out of his chair like a shot, kicked it over behind him, and made a lunge for Enderby. He called him some more fancy names and I managed to get in between them, and Henry got hold of Frank's arm. At least that got Enderby on his feet! But I will say he didn't turn a hair. The two fellows at the drafting table had stopped work and seemed to be enjoying the show.

" 'Better let me handle this,' I told Frank, and I turned back to Enderby. I told him he might better deal his cards face up about the reclamation district and his connection with it, if he had any. He said, 'All right,' cool as ever. 'This is for the record,' he said. 'I am not chief engineer of any reclamation district here or elsewhere. I never have been. The government employed me to survey the water potentials of this valley and make a report. I've done so. This report is in Washington. If you people jumped to conclusions, it's not my fault.'

"It seemed to me that was debatable, but I let it pass. I thought of asking him what was in that report, but I let that go by, too. So, next, I put it to him straight from the shoulder. Was Los Angeles up here for a water supply? He looked me in the eye and said, 'Yes.' That was all. Just 'yes.'

" 'That'll be a big job,' I said, hoping to draw him out. I drew him out all right. For the first time the fellow showed some sign of interest that was almost human. He leaned forward and raised his voice a shade. 'Big enough,' he said. 'The biggest project any city has ever undertaken. Taking water from eternal snows three hundred miles over deserts and across mountain ranges. It'll capture the imagination of the civilized world.' You'd have thought he was a born orator to hear him."

John gave an explosive sigh and stared moodily toward the mountains with their eternal snows that this man would lead away to the distant city.

"That's just the trouble, Abbie," he went on dejectedly. "It *will* capture public imagination. Nobody will think about a handful of backwoods ranchers or what it's going to do to them." He shook his head. "I had all I wanted, but I guess Frank hadn't. He got up out of his chair again and looked down at Enderby.

" 'You've told us a lot,' he said. 'So we haven't got a reclamation district, we never had one, and if we had you weren't connected with it. That makes a liar out of you for my money because I've heard you say otherwise. But I've got one more question. If you don't represent us, or the government, who the hell do you represent?'

56

"Enderby put his pipe back in his mouth and said, cold as a dead salmon, 'The city of Los Angeles.'"

When I stirred, my limbs felt stiff and old. It was like coming out of a bad dream, only not far enough out. I saw how weary John looked, and I bottled up all the feeling that surged up in me, and said as commonplacely as I could, "What you need is a cup of good strong, hot tea."

John's eyes met mine squarely and the ghost of a smile touched them. "More than that!" He managed a grin. "A couple of good murders would help."

The light pouring through the windows pointed up the white at his temples and picked out the lines in his forehead. As I passed the sofa, he reached out and caught my arm. I took his hand and brought it to my cheek, pressing it hard. Then I went out to the kitchen to make the tea.

Chapter 5.

THE vast evening shadow of the Sierra marched across the valley, its hues of heather advancing almost perceptibly as the last golden sunshine lying on the broad lowlands faded before it. Already the somber fingers of night reached out to touch our ranch and the homes of our neighbors.

I had always loved this brief period of phantom colors which were neither of the day nor of the night, stealing so softly over meadows and orchards and the gray reaches of sage, mellowing the mountain silhouettes and the stern contours of the Alabama Hills. But this evening, as John talked to me, the dusk that dimmed all Golden Valley and crept upon us where we sat, seemed ominous. To have an end of it, as I brought back our tea to the darkening room, I resolutely lit the lamp on the table. And then another, beside the door, for one seemed not bright enough to defeat the gloom.

"Now," I said presently, "tell me the rest."

John set down his empty cup.

"Back at Will Fiske's office," he continued, "Frank was all for starting lawsuits, until Will made it clear there was nothing to sue about. We finally decided that all we could do was to wait for developments. Will would keep watch at Bishop. Henry and I were to travel round the country to learn what was actually going on and try to rouse the ranchers to their danger.

"We all thought Frank ought to go along, as people might talk more freely to him than us. But he balked. Said he had to get back to Independence and start building his fences. Henry flared up and reminded him that he had a bigger stake involved than any of us. The odd thing was that Frank, so hot-headed, took that all right.

" 'That's just it,' he said. 'Everything I got this valley gave me. You all know how I came here, twenty-five years ago, stone broke. You recollect how I started. Shepherding, cowpunching, mine-mucking, teaming. All the time I kept saving a little money till I had enough to start a store. That panned out good, and after a while I sold out and started the bank. Did it on a shoestring, but it paid out, too, and I've enjoyed it. Maybe it ain't what you'd call good banking—but I've kinda liked helping people along when they were up against it. And I haven't lost much that way, either! Now, my valley's in a fight. It's going to be a tough fight; don't make any mistake about that. The dirtiest we ever got into. I'd just like you all to know I'm in it till the last chip is down. But I got to get my stack together, first.'

"With that," John said, "he walked right out. It'll be a

long time, Abbie, before I forget that little speech of his."

From then on John and Henry put in long days driving from ranch to ranch, talking to those who had already optioned and those who hadn't. They talked to ranchers who depended on seepage water. Those who had optioned were afraid the options wouldn't be exercised, and John said it was not surprising; they were getting three times the normal value of their land. Those who hadn't optioned greeted the callers like brothers, thinking they were land buyers. "They aren't fighting *anybody*, Abbie," John groaned. "They're selling—if the City will buy. It's like a fever and it's already got a hold. . . ."

"What about the seepage land people?" I asked.

"They don't seem worried," John shrugged. "They're looking for land buyers, too. I found only one fellow awake to what's really happening. Youngster, name of Wilkins. Got a pretty girl wife. Both of them were half crazy from worry."

The evening shadows deepened, the mountains turned purple. A soft wind began to rustle the cottonwood leaves.

"They'd reason to be," he said presently. "They don't have a drop of water of their own. Most of the ranches we visited don't. If this Los Angeles scheme goes through, over half the ranches in this valley will be dried up and their owners ruined."

So there was the threat that lay over our land—the threat that the desert would come creeping back to reclaim the fair acres we had taken from it, the desert whose uncompromising cruelties we knew so well. No gold was ever so precious as the water we would lose. All our sacrifice and toil of the past years would be wasted in the vaster waste of this desert. The immensity of the tragedy as it was measured by those of us who must live with it, kept me silent.

I saw John lie back and close his eyes. I crossed the room between my chair and John. Stooping, I touched my lips to his cheek. He did not open his eyes, but a little sound, half tenderness, half groan, moved his throat.

"We'll fight them, John," I whispered foolishly, tears in my eyes. "Fight and win, too! We're not of the giving-in stuff. Go upstairs now to bed. You can snatch a few winks before supper. To please me, John. . . ."

Again it was late afternoon and I was in my rose garden. Cold water chuckled through the little ditches that crisscrossed the neat beds, the deeper voice of the main ditch a throaty gurgle. These days I seemed acutely aware of water—its sound, its sparkle, its vitality.

Looking up, I saw Abby walking up the path toward me. She was dressed for riding and swung her sombrero by its tasseled chin strap. As she drew nearer I was struck by the look on her face. It was as though I were seeing two faces framed in one. Her mouth was gentle, soft, and with a hint of smile to lift its corners; her eyes were somber and brooding, vaguely resentful.

"I've been out to see David," she announced, throwing herself down on a bench and fanning with her hat.

"In this heat?" I protested.

"Why not?" She looked surprised. "Inyo sun never hurt anyone."

"How is David?"

"All right." She looked over the hatbrim at me. "He's in love with me—and I am with him." But there was no lilt in her voice.

"Heavens, child!" I sat down beside her. "How do you know?" They had met all of ten days before.

"He didn't *tell* me. He isn't that sort, Hanny. Besides, he didn't need to. We both have known. Right along, I expect." She reached into a pocket and fished out a smudged slip of paper. "Look at that."

I scanned the paper, squinting without my glasses.

"From Abby in an old-fashioned black velvet gown North 26° 27′ 33″ West 562.43 ft. to Abby in a blue dress that just matches her eyes."

"What on earth is this?" I demanded.

"David Allen's way of making love."

"It seems a bit . . . impersonal," I suggested.

She laughed a little. "When I say something like that, David reminds me he's an engineer." Then she gently took her precious bit of paper from me. "You see, I went out and boldly hunted him up. He talked a lot of nonsense about my face getting into the lens of his transit and shutting off the flag!" She looked childishly proud of her surveyor's jargon. "He wondered what they'd say in the office if he sent in a field note like this." She looked at the paper, then thrust it into her pocket.

"We laughed about it and I asked him to make a copy for me. We were sitting under an old scraggly Joshua, the only shade there was for a mile. He'd sent his men on ahead." She sighed. "The work never stops. Then he
62

looked up at the Joshua and made a kind of bow. 'Howdy, Brer Joshuay,' he said. 'How wuz them walls of Jericho, last time you seen 'em?'

"That got me to thinking of our Joshua trees and how the Indians light them when somebody dies and how they look like candles in the night, stretching out across the valley. All of a sudden, thinking that way, Hanny, I felt choked up inside. I told David about it, the Indians' ceremony and all.

"He sat there on a hard boulder staring out across the desert at the dust devils whirling the crazy way they do. He said it must be a sight to see the Joshuas burning, and then he looked at me—I can't describe the look, Hanny—and he said, 'This country means a lot to you, doesn't it?'"

Abby closed her eyes and sighed.

"Of course, I told him how much I loved it. If you can really put anything like that into words. Then, we started talking about . . . water." She tipped her sunny head down, studying her boots.

"We simply didn't get anywhere, Hanny," she said miserably. "David can't see anything wrong in Los Angeles buying the water it needs when people are willing to sell. I tried to tell him how we looked at Golden Valley as our own—how we'd had to fight the Indians, Nature, and outlaws to hold it. I told him all about us! How you'd worked and planned. I told him about the long, awful trip and about Uncle Amos and Aunt Susan and Uncle David. He was sweet and understanding. Yet, he *didn't* understand at all, because he came right back and said there ought to be enough water for everybody."

She flung her head up and looked at me and her eyes were full of tears.

"I had to give up, Hanny," she went on. "I wouldn't talk about it any more. But that didn't help. Both of us knew the thing was right there, grinning at us. And it always will be there! I was so choked up I couldn't talk and I don't think he felt much better. So I came home. But the last thing I saw, Hanny, was David standing there, under that old Joshua. . . ." She buried her head in her hat and I stroked her hair and patted her shoulder with idiotic little pats that couldn't help anything, let alone a young girl with a troubled heart!

That night I told John about Abby and David.

"Poor youngsters," he said. "They may have a rough road ahead of them."

"He could quit his job," I suggested.

"You know better, Abbie. He couldn't do that. Not till he's convinced about the crowd he's signed up with. Let's not forget that Los Angeles does have its side."

"*Its* side?"

"Yes, *its* side. Look at it. They're buying, not taking. They're paying big prices. They've got to have water. Everybody knows that. This looks like a good place to get it. Of course, people will sell *because they want* to, Abbie, not because they're being forced off their land. I can understand how young Allen looks at it. Most everybody except us will look at it that way, too.

"Listen to this," he went on. "Will Fiske wired Harry Sansene right off." Harry was our Congressman. "This is what he got back: Nobody in Washington admits ever

hearing of a reclamation district in Golden Valley. He
went to the President. *He* hadn't heard about it, either.
But he *had* heard about Los Angeles, and lectured Harry
for twenty minutes about the greatest good to the greatest
number. That last is an exact quotation of the President's
words.

"The cold fact is that L.A. hasn't missed a trick. I don't
know how, but they used the government to get their
preliminary work done and drew a red herring in front
of us in the form of this fake reclamation district. Another
cold fact is that we've nobody but ourselves to blame. I
did a lot of digging, Abbie, and I can't find a solitary soul
who ever heard of Enderby or anybody else come out
flatfooted and say they were working on a district. We did
just jump to a conclusion."

The last sunset fires had died on the Inyos and night
already was purple on the eastern hills beyond.

"Don't take it too hard, dear." John laid a comforting arm
on my shoulder. "We aren't licked. Indeed, I think we've
got a good chance. The first thing is to stiffen the people
against selling. The best way to do that is to make it
pretty plain what it'll do to their neighbors. When Los
Angeles does come into the open, then we'll fall back on
Will Fiske. As for Abby and David Allen—they won't be
the only ones in this valley who will have problems."

David came to Sunday dinner. For a few hours the
house was filled with music and laughter though there
were sudden silences.

65

Once for a few moments David found me alone. "You know I love Abby," he said abruptly.

"She told me something of it."

"I suppose she told you how my job seems to stand between us."

I nodded.

"Abby means more to me than anything," he said hurriedly. "But this business just seems to go round in circles. I have an idea that might help everybody, us included." He frowned, feeling for the right words.

"Tell me."

"Los Angeles has never met with you folks, or you with Los Angeles. I know Angus MacAndrew, our chief engineer. He's absolutely square, Mrs. Weston. I know that for a fact. He was my dad's closest friend. I think there are a lot of things up here he doesn't know about. I think he . . . ought to know about them." He looked at me, pleadingly.

"Well?" I said.

"I'd like to get him up here, if you think it will be all right. I'd like to have him talk things over with Mr. Weston and any others you want. I think he'd come if I asked him to and told him some of the things I've heard."

"By all means," I said. "Tell him we'd like to have him stop with us."

Chapter 6.

THE last extension leaf had been put into the table; Mark, Peter, and Little John were there, just down from the high mountains with the cattle. John had asked Frank Masters, Paul Gideon, and Will Fiske. Then there were ourselves—Henry, Joan, Carrol, Abby, and I. David came with Angus MacAndrew.

According to David, it was MacAndrew who had envisioned a water supply for his city to be taken from our valley and its mountain; he who had translated his dream into plans that feasibly could overcome apparently insurmountable obstacles; he who had persuaded sometimes hostile, and always doubtful, officials that his plan should be undertaken.

MacAndrew was a big man, big of frame and of voice and gifted of a dry Scotch wit that brought laughter to us all, though, at heart, we were anything but gay. Even Gim Lee in the kitchen could be heard cackling shrilly and attempting snatches of garbled mimicry for Mary's benefit.

Angus MacAndrew had started as a hard-rock miner as we could see by the blue powder marks on his face and hands. From there he had climbed to shift boss, then to foreman. But construction beckoned and he soon quit his mining. We all laughed with him over his struggles with a correspondence course that in the end opened the way to construction engineering.

"I learned," he said, "but only after sweat and tribulation. These paws o' mine"—he held up his two great hands for all to see—"were na meant for copyin' exameenation papers."

As places were found in the sitting room after dinner, we seemed to have grouped ourselves instinctively, Mr. MacAndrew in a big chair beside the window, with David flanking him, and the rest of us facing the two. MacAndrew chuckled as he noted the arrangement.

"In battle array a'ready. 'Tis a bit early, still. . . ." He laughed again resoundingly. John started to move, but MacAndrew checked him.

"Na, na, man," he said. "Whatever deefferences we may uncover will no be heightened by reason of our seatin'. Let's have at it. The lad here"—he jerked his rugged chin toward David—"tells me I'm on th' way to raise th' deil an a' wi' you good people up here. I'd know more about it. Suppose ye tell me." He looked at John.

"That won't take long," John answered, and told him what had been learned, both through our own investigation and directly from Mr. Enderby.

MacAndrew listened attentively, his face expressionless.

"Naturally we've no intention of sitting idly by and seeing our water taken from us," John concluded.

MacAndrew made no answer, frowning and rubbing his chin.

"No," he said at length, "answerin' your first conclusion I wouldna expect you would, although I canna agree to your claim o' possession. As individuals, what water ye own is yours, of course, and ye may do with it as ye see fit—use it, or sell it, or give it away. But as a community asset, na." He smiled a bleak smile that held no hint of compromise. "This valley has been here long. There has been no pooling of its water resources that I know of."

"What do you call our reclamation district?" Frank Masters demanded.

MacAndrew shook his great head. "Not until the lad here told me, have I heard aught of any reclamation district in this valley. And Mr. Weston, I tell ye plain, here and now, that neither I nor my department had any talk wi' Washington, nor have I heard of any. I did not know that Jim Enderby was retained to make preliminary exameenations of water potentials. I regarded him as a good man and okayed him. I thought he was honest. Having made some investigation of my own, after hearin' from Davie lad, I found out otherwise. He's fired."

MacAndrew turned his broad palms up, then laid them flatly upon his knees.

"The noo," he went on, "I'll tell ye more. Being employed by a great city in desperate need of water, I dreamed a dream wherein I found my city's salvation in this valley. But it was three hundred miles away. Between us

69

and here were deserts and mountains. So I turned all the wits I had toward surmounting Nature's obstacles, leaving preliminaries to others, never doubting for one minute that whatever we got we'd pay for, all fair and square."

"There are things you can't measure in dollars and cents, MacAndrew," John pointed out. But MacAndrew's retort was quick.

"I wouldna say water was one of 'em when the owner was willin' to sell."

"They're willing enough at treble prices," Frank Masters growled.

"Paid for or not, treble prices or not, the fact remains that you're taking water out of this valley," John said, his voice rising with impatience. "And that's something we have no intention of permitting if we can help ourselves."

MacAndrew nodded. "Cleanly put, sir. I'll be equally frank. I'm of no mind to see a city of a third of a million souls go thirsty when there's water in sight and to spare. Ye've repeatedly called it 'our water.' I wouldna call water that runs to waste the private property of onybody."

"Waste?" John echoed. "What do you mean?"

"Just this," MacAndrew answered imperturbably. "Wi' me own eyes I've seen thousands of inches of water pourin' into your river and from there emptyin' into that sinkhole of soda, alkali, and God-knows-what that ye call Owens Lake. If that's no sinfu' waste I never saw it."

"Which in turn justifies Los Angeles in coming up here and taking what it wants?" Will Fiske asked.

"Buying, not taking. Ye could have the Mississippi

flowin' through this valley and into that lake and Los Angeles would hae no legal right to touch it. The time will come when, to hold water, ye must make use of it. But that time is no here yet. So—we buy what we need and can get."

"Then we're to understand that Los Angeles intends to carry through this project regardless?" John asked quietly.

"Aye," MacAndrew replied.

John drew a deep breath. "That being the case," he said, "there doesn't appear to be much more to discuss. We're obliged to you, Mr. MacAndrew, for coming to see us. We're obliged to you for your frankness and straight talk."

MacAndrew inclined his head gravely. "Aye. But as to their being no more to discuss, I differ."

John looked at him curiously. "Yes?"

MacAndrew rubbed his jaw reflectively.

"Davie tells me that some of your best ranches are watered solely by seepage, and own no water of their own. That any that abutt upon streams we've bought, and from which we'll some day be takin' the water, will thereby be dried up and ruined. I'd know more about that, and mainly the whys."

"You're unaware of the geological formation of this valley?" John asked.

"I've had mostly to concern myself with the surface, not what's beneath it."

"Briefly put, here it is," John explained. "The streams come down from the steep mountains over granite. When

71

they reach the level of the valley and leave the granite, naturally their velocity slows. Their water seeps into the porous ground. Subterranean channels pick it up and carry it far away from the parent streams, sometimes as much as two or three miles. But it keeps pushing up to the surface again subirrigating thousands of acres. You've seen our meadows and orchards?"

MacAndrew nodded.

"It makes the finest crop land we have," John went on. "I can show ranch after ranch that hasn't a drop of water of its own and yet has so much surface water that they have to ditch it off to work it. Seepage is the life of our valley, Mr. MacAndrew. If you cut it off at its source, then half this valley will go back to desert."

MacAndrew made a vague rumbling sound. "And such ranches Los Angeles is na buyin'?"

"Exactly."

"And naught is being done to compensate the owners?"

"Not that I'm aware of."

MacAndrew thought for a moment, then said dryly, "We'll see about that. Ye'll understand, though, that the land buyin' is no in my hands. I'm the ditchdigger. And ye'll understand this as well. I make no promises. I couldna be sure of keepin' 'em if I did. But I'm no buildin' my drreams on broken hearts and broken fortunes."

He stared moodily at one of his great hands.

"I'm bound to warn ye all, though, that a big city is a complex creature. 'Tis a thing of fractions and cliques, of jealousy and greed, of hidden tides and sudden whirl-pools. No honest man controls or owns it. He would na be honest if he did." He shook his head and sighed. "I'm spendin' thirty millions o' dollars o' taxpayers' money on this drream o' mine—more, probably, before it's done. I'd surrender ten years of my life to give the people thirty millions of value. I never will. From the votin' booth to the last shovelful of dirt I'll be stole blind, and I'll no be able to stop it." He looked slowly round our circle.

"I say all this that ye may know what I'll be up against. I told ye I'd make no promises. I take that back. There's one I will make, and keep. I'll do the verra best I can for those ye speak of."

MacAndrew and David were gone. MacAndrew had declined our offer of hospitality, saying that he would like to spend a night or two in camp with his men just for old times' sake.

John looked at the boys, a compact trio, standing together.

"Well, what do you think of it?"

Mark, spokesman for the three, said gruffly, "Bad. That fellow will do his best to be fair, but Los Angeles comes first."

"Blast his fairness!" Frank Masters broke out angrily. "Let's carry the fight to him."

"How would you go about it?" John demanded.

"File injunction suits. Sue 'em for conspiracy. Sue 'em for anything and everything. Arrest their men for trespass."

"Oh, Frank, for heaven's sake!" Will snapped exasperatedly.

"Then why don't you offer something?" Frank retorted.

John turned to the boys again. "What do you suggest?" he asked.

Mark shook his head. "Nothing. We don't know enough about it. Besides, we're cattlemen, Pete and I, and the Injun's about half and half. The way I see it, this is a fight between the ranchers and Los Angeles. We cowmen aren't in on it. We'll do anything you tell us, but a cowman can't ever get a rancher's angle. I'd say you go ahead and boss it, Dad. Do what you think best. That right, boys?"

Peter and Little John nodded.

"All we can do now," John continued, "is to try to stiffen people against selling."

"Lot of good that'll do with L.A. offering such fancy prices," Frank grumbled.

"You're likely right. But it's the only thing until Los Angeles actually starts taking water. We'd have something to go on then, wouldn't we, Will?"

"If they don't get some made-to-order laws passed in the meantime," Will answered unhappily.

Chapter 7.

I KNEW just how it must be—as well as if I were with John on those trips. Faint desert roads, mere wheel tracks, leading to lonely ranches and struggling homesteads. First heat, then cold that turned to wind, rain, sleet, and snow. Iron-shod wheels grinding eternally through coarse desert gravel. Blinding clouds of soda and alkali. Hours spent in patient, detailed explanation, going over and over the same point, leaving it only to return to it and stress it again. Friendly talks and others not so friendly.

Desert folk are unlike any others, I think. Their affairs are rigidly their own, not to be pried into. And John *must* pry. He must talk. Most difficult of all, he must explain to those who saw sudden wealth within their grasp why their good fortune was bound to spell ruin for their neighbors and desolation for their valley. And always he must be alert against fatal acts of violence by the hotheads.

In all those weeks it was a comfort to know that Henry

was always with John. I could picture him, saying little, sitting through discussions held in yard or barn or house. But he was there, a sturdy sounding board against which John might the better weigh the fruits of his effort.

In the brief periods when John was at home, he was so tired that he was glad to sit, silent and relaxed, in his favorite chair, his hands dangling at his sides.

"Folks are queer, Abbie," he said. "The ones you'd bank on will hardly talk to you. The ones you'd swear would be hostile aren't at all."

I had dug up some crocheting from an old trunk to keep my hands from fidgeting these days, and I worked at it as John talked. I had almost forgotten what it was to have nerves in our years of quiet and plenty.

"People are full of surprises," I agreed, not very brightly.

"Most of them just flatly won't believe me. Others think something—they don't know what!—will turn up to fix everything. Then there are those that are frankly hungry for easy money. They make me the maddest. Nearly everyone I've talked to is well fixed. I'd understand some poor devil who hadn't made a go of it getting out. But they're the very ones that'll stick."

Whenever Abby spent a Sunday with us, David was on hand. At these times there was laughter and lightness, but the lightness was often subdued, and I had a feeling that the laughter lay no deeper than the lips.

Once, when I had her to myself, I said to Abby, "You're eating your hearts out. Both of you!"

"It's not any fun, Hanny," she admitted soberly. "There just isn't anything we can do about it."

"Seize your happiness," I counseled as I had once before, and took her hand in mine. But she only shook her head and looked away. I felt a vehement protest rise in me at her first love's being dragged through a sordid business dispute.

"There are other places than here," I suggested, but I couldn't help faltering over it a little. I couldn't picture little Abby of the sun-dappled hair and straight shoulders anywhere but in the valley. "David's profession is everywhere."

"That would be running away, Hanny," she pointed out sadly. "Neither of us would be willing to do that. We . . . haven't even talked about it."

"But you can't go on this way."

"I'm afraid we have no choice. I told you we'd be on opposite sides—and we are. Maybe we're both right, or both wrong. I don't know. All I do know is that we love each other. I . . . I guess that kind of keeps us going." She gave me a sudden kiss, and went away.

As I sat, staring hard at the mountains, the warmth of her soft lips still on my cheek, my plan was born.

John decided to hold community meetings.

"It will give the folks a chance to ask questions and air their views and talk to each other," he said.

Of necessity such gatherings were held at night in schoolhouses, halls, churches, and homes, giving John more travel, work, and late hours. He always gave me an opportunity to go along, but I begged off until the big meeting at Independence.

77

"They may not come this far south," John said, "but young Allen's outfit is still at work up George's Creek and I'm taking no chances. We'll get the valley organized as far as Lone Pine, anyhow. I don't think we need worry about anything farther south."

Between Lone Pine and Olancha was Cottonwood Creek, the finest stream in the valley, with Cottonwood Ranch at its mouth. The Espinozas owned the ranch. Below there was only barren desert stretching on to Cartago and Olancha, and all the water there was owned by our boys and Fritz Aber. Certainly Los Angeles would never see the day it could even talk to Mark, Peter, and Little John. And dynamite couldn't have blown Fritz off his fair ranch.

"I make her!" he used to say, glowing. "I'm goin' to die on her."

There was one other ranch still farther south—Haiwee, a sunken spring-fed meadow. There was nothing about Haiwee to attract Los Angeles, and if there had been they would still have had Nora Hansen to deal with. Nora was tall, rawboned, and belligerent, with eyes like Scandinavian ice.

The night of the meeting at Independence saw snow clouds piling in over the western mountains and spreading out across the valley. A bilious moon shone dimly through them. A cold north wind, straight from the snows of Mono, blustered down Main Street, driving dust and leaves and old papers before it.

The hall was already packed when we got there, its atmosphere hot and close. A faint crackle of applause greeted John as he made his way toward the speakers' table, and I was proud of him and the part he was playing as we were shown to the places that had been held for us.

I settled myself as comfortably as I could in the uncompromising chair, and looked around. John was shaking hands with the committee members. I counted them off: Frank Masters, Will Fiske from Bishop; George Benedict, a cowman in stained mackinaw and embroidered high-heeled boots; Frank Lebert and Frank Lazzini, sheepmen; Paul Gideon and George McAfee, merchants; Judge Hunter, Jose Rico, withered and blue-jeaned but one of the richest men in the valley; Henry and Tom Ellison.

They were all respected men of substance, representing Independence, Lone Pine, Manzanar, and Eight Mile. Bishop and Big Pine had already had their meetings. That night's gathering rounded out the organization of the valley against the threat that hung over it.

My eyes went over the audience—ranchers, merchants, stockmen, homesteaders, miners, and a sprinkling of Indians who had doubtless been persuaded to come by Little John.

My look lingered longest on the faces of the women. So many of them had aged long before their time, for our land was cruel to those who sought to tame it. Their hands were as gnarled as those of the men, but they had groped toward some adornment—a ribbon in lifeless hair, an old brooch, a bonnet that may have been cherished for a decade, a worn dress painstakingly mended and pressed.

In a far corner I saw a colorless little man. At first my gaze brushed over him until I realized that over one ear

79

was a black disk held in place by a metal clamp that went over the head. A slight start shot through me. This, then, would be the man Bushnell. An open notebook rested on his knee, and directly behind him was Little John. Little John's opaque eyes were fixed upon the speakers' table, but I knew that Bushnell would make no move and write no word but would be seen and catalogued by those sharp black eyes.

I remembered then that John, when talking of this unpleasant stranger, had wondered if Bushnell was actually deaf or merely pretended to be to make it easier at times to overhear conversation that might prove helpful. It was true, John said, that when Bushnell was walking about or drinking in a saloon, he did not wear his hearing device, but put it on only when he was seated or engaged in a conversation. Other times, if spoken to, he would apologize for his infirmity in the flat, toneless voice of the deaf.

"I wouldn't be a bit surprised," John had said, "if the slippery devil can hear as well as I can."

Little John, hovering about at the time, had grunted, "One day we find out." I didn't doubt he was at work right then.

In crisp, plain words John told what Los Angeles proposed to do and what would come if it succeeded. From there he went straight to the need for organization at once if the city was to be stopped before it was too late. Bluntly he told how we had been balked in our fine reclamation plans, but laid no blame anywhere, although he did say that it might be a matter of general interest to know that James Enderby was no longer in Golden Valley.

80

John spoke to the people in their own language, and while he talked there was not a sound in the hall except the heavy breathing of the listeners.

When he had finished, there was a moment of absolute silence. Then someone began to clap and immediately the applause grew to an enthusiastic roar of sound. From somewhere in the back of the building came a wild, "Ki yippy yippy!," the turbulent cry that had sent the longhorns surging up the Chisholm Trail and citizens scurrying for cover in Abilene, Dodge City, and a dozen other frontier towns. Chills of pride and excitement chased each other up and down my spine. Golden Valley was still frontier, as the trespasser would discover.

John smilingly held up a hand.

"All right," he said, when at last the tumult had died down. "It would seem we're pretty much of a mind." This brought out a fresh outburst. "The meeting's yours. I've told you what's ahead," he added when he could make himself heard. "Anybody that has ideas, let's have 'em."

There was some stir and whispering, and finally Fred Lindstrom stood up. He was a tall, gaunt man with far-away Scandinavian eyes, and he owned a fine ranch near Eight Mile with a stream of water running through the heart of it. Everybody knew and liked Fred Lindstrom.

"Ay got von qvestion ay vant to ask, Yon," he said.

"All right. Let's have it, Fred."

"It bane dis. Suppose a feller he come in vit de rest, den maybe some day he vant to sell. How about dot?"

A voice shouted roughly from the back of the hall, "No!" There was a rustling and a craning of necks.

81

"A man can always sell what's his own," John said promptly. "Coming into the Defense Committee doesn't bind you to anything. It only shows Los Angeles that we're standing together." He paused and pressed his hand upon the table. "There is only this about it, Fred," he continued, "and it applies to you or anybody who may be thinking the same question. These days it will be a good idea to know who you're selling to. You've got neighbors to think about."

"Else they might start thinking about you, Lindstrom." The interruption was once more from the back of the room, harsh and menacing.

"Vell, it bane a feller's own ranch," Fred persisted.

"You're right," John answered crisply. "I told you nobody was bound by anything but his own conscience. Anything else, Fred?"

"No, tank you, Yon." Fred sat down again, at once the center of a buzz of whispering. Gradually his face turned a deep red and he squared himself away to look fixedly at John and the committee, ignoring the fierce whispers.

A young man stood up, a clean-cut, nice-looking young fellow. Beside him sat a pretty young woman with a baby in her arms. I had never seen them before.

"Maybe you remember me, Mr. Weston," the man said half shyly. "My name is Wilkins. You and the other gentleman"—he nodded toward Henry—"stopped in to see me up at Bishop."

"So we did, Mr. Wilkins. Glad to have you with us." John smiled at the young man. "Something on your mind?"

"Yes, sir. When you talked to me everything seemed

82

pretty clear. Then other people talked and no two seemed to say the same thing. What I'd like to know is just where seepage ranches will be if this Los Angeles scheme does go through?"

"Dried to a crisp," John answered grimly. He looked about the suddenly quiet room. "Maybe I didn't make that point clear enough. Such ranches—seepage ones, I mean—don't own any water or water rights. They've been watered by underground seepage from adjacent streams. If the water is flumed or piped out of those streams, which Los Angeles will undoubtedly do with every one it controls, they'll become dried-up ranches. Is that clear to everybody?"

Young Wilkins' tanned face drained white, and I saw his wife's hand go to her throat in a gesture of fear and helplessness.

"Yes, sir, it's clear to me," Wilkins said and sat down.

Another man stood up. He was Harry Brewer, known as a trouble-maker. "What sort of a fight you figurin' on putting up?" he demanded now in a truculent voice. His face was flushed, as though he had been drinking.

"If you ask me that personally," John answered, his voice even, "I don't know. That's for the committee to decide. Bishop, Big Pine, Independence, and Lone Pine will each pick its own local committee. The main Central Committee will be selected from that. It will plan how we shall fight and when."

"I can tell you how to do the job right now," Harry growled. "Run 'em out at the point of sixshooters."

83

There was so much cheering that John was obliged to pound the table with his gavel.

"And bring the militia in on us," he shouted. The noise ebbed away and eyes, tense and curious, were turned from Harry to John. "I'm not the committee," John stated flatly. "But if I have anything to do with it, I tell you, Harry Brewer, and everybody in this room, there is going to be no violence, no shooting. We'll fight as hard as God will let us, but we'll not play into the other fellow's hands. The thing they'd like best is for us to break the law. Then everyone would be against us."

There were a few dissenting calls mingled with the approving voices. Harry Brewer sat down with an angry face. I saw someone, I couldn't tell who, lean over and pat him on the back. Then Jane Calkins stood up.

Jane was known and liked by everyone. We all admired her brave struggle to wrest a livelihood out of her meagerly subirrigated homestead.

"Who is going to head this Central Committee, Mr. Weston?" she asked.

John smiled. "I don't know, Mrs. Calkins. The committee will select its own chairman."

She thought this over for a moment, her head a little on one side, the cords of her thin neck distended.

"We-ell," she said, "if it's going to be you, I'll do anything I can. If it's somebody else, I'm not very hopeful."

A tumult of applause answered her. As John kept rapping vainly for order, Will Fiske pushed his way to the front, holding his hands up for quiet.

"Speaking for Bishop and Big Pine, John Weston is chairman right now!" he shouted.

"That goes for Independence!" Frank Masters bellowed.

"We ain't had no meeting at Lone Pine," someone shouted, "and we don't need none. John Weston's good enough for us."

John's forehead was flushed and moist now, and he mopped it vigorously. "That's nice of you all," he said as soon as he could make himself heard. "But I'm still going to leave it to the committee."

There followed more general talk, a few more questions asked. Then under John's deft steering the local committee was appointed: John, Henry, Tom Ellison, Frank Masters, Paul Gideon, Frank Lebert, Jose Rico, George Benedict, Frank Lazzini, and George McAfee.

Just as the people were beginning to make their way out, Harry Brewer pushed through the crowd and confronted John.

"Now, this ain't anything against you, John," he blustered, "but I'm telling you I'm going to fight my own way."

"All right, Harry," John replied calmly. "Only remember one thing. You could hurt a lot of people."

Snow was falling steadily as we drove home—a fairy curtain that veiled the world, whitened the road, and muffled the hoofbeats and the sound of wheels. I was full of a mixture of feelings. The uneasiness I had been unable to shake off since the day David Allen walked into my house and away with Abby's heart; pride in my husband who, after all the homeliness of our long years together,

85

could still stir me to adoration; fear of the plan that lay in my mind day and night; and an unwelcome weariness of the flesh that cried out to the fighting spirit still in me: *Let it all alone! Let the others take care of this. You've fought enough. You're getting old. Rest and enjoy the peace you have earned.*

But John was older than I. He had looked heartbreakingly weary for weeks, yet had not given in. His unselfishness moved me to shame. How could I dream in my rocker with my backward gaze on mountain and desert while the valley we had made became parched and perished?

I snuggled a little closer to John, and my hand groped until it found his and clung.

Chapter 8.

I FRETTED no end about telling John of Uncle Amos' gold, the secret I had kept from him so long. But I need not have worried. John listened closely to my anxious telling of the story; and when I had finished, he was silent for a time, holding in his hand the Mint Certificates while I braced myself for his disapproval.

"For a woman," he said whimsically, "you keep a secret moderately well, Abbie. I must say this was a jolt at first. There have been times when that money *would* have come in handy."

How well I knew that; and the memory of some of those times brought tears to my eyes, although I think they came partly in relief that at last my secret was shared.

"Don't do that, my dear. Please." John's quiet voice made me feel guilty all over again.

"I should have told you," I all but wailed.

"No, you shouldn't," he disagreed. "It was the old man's money. He was entitled to have it handled any way he wanted." He bent over and kissed the top of my head. "Now, stop crying and tell me more about what you're figuring on."

Somehow I fumbled through my plan, although as I talked it seemed far from the clever thing I had first visualized. There were gaps that had never before revealed themselves to me, weaknesses that made the whole thing seem no more than a woman's romantic fantasy. But John sat quietly through my stumbling recital, watching me intently. When I had finished, he turned so that he could look out the window, as though he had a need to see our valley whose future we were so fearful of.

At last he turned back to me, fixing his eyes gravely upon my face.

"It's a pretty big idea," he said. "You can do a lot with money, including losing it. Who's going to handle this thing for you? One thing is certain: neither you nor I can appear in it."

"Why?"

"Because I'm chairman of the committee. If either of us starts throwing money around, it will be laid square at the committee's door. Every fellow who is hard up will come to us. When we turn him down, as we'd mostly have to do, the committee would be in bad. Right away half the people in the valley would hate us and the other half wouldn't trust us."

"But *I'm* not a member of any committee."

"No," John admitted with a smile. "You just happen to be my wife. That'd be all they'd need."

I was stunned to silence. All that had appeared relatively simple in my thoughts now was beset with pitfalls.

"I hadn't expected to take part . . . actively," I explained with my eyes in my lap. "I intended having David Allen do it for me."

John's look of surprise broke into noisy mirth.

"Lord, Abbie," he groaned. "You're beyond me. Not enough, is it, to be Lady Bountiful? You've got to play Cupid as well!" He bit his laughter off, his face hardened. "You haven't forgotten that he works for the other side?"

"No," I said mutinously, "and I want to get him away from them and everything that has to do with the city! I want him to have honest work so he can hold his head up. And I don't want to see those children eat their hearts out." I fidgeted nervously with the front of my dress, pinching it into little pleats and smoothing them out again.

"Just a minute, Abbie." John's face was sober but his eyes smiled. "That's pretty strong talk. I'd say young Allen considers his work honest enough as it is. As to holding his head up, I haven't noticed him doing any slinking. It's all fine about helping those two kids get together but I have a notion they'll want to handle that their own way. What's more, I'm pretty sure that young fellow won't quit his job until he sees some good reason."

"Good reason?" I cried. "What better reason than that he works for the city?"

"To you, none. It's just possible he might think differently. However, go ahead and try him. But first, get organized. Go up and see Will Fiske. Tell him what you want to do and ask him how to do it. Explain about young Allen.

89

And tell him that you and I are not to appear in any way."

He took my hand in his. "A while ago you were being hard on yourself, Abbie girl," he said tenderly. "And unnecessarily. You did exactly right. Now forget it. I shall."

Will Fiske took off his spectacles and wiped them with elaborate care.

"So you kept it a secret all these years," he said. "How did John take it?"

My heart warmed at the memory. "He said I did exactly right."

"That sounds like John Weston," Will agreed. "He's right, too, about neither of you being mixed up in it. Anybody in mind to run it for you?"

I asked him if he thought the plan was practical and if real good could be done through it.

"Yes," Will replied thoughtfully. "Yes, to both questions. Its practicality depends upon who handles it. So does the good that can be accomplished. What you're really setting up is a sort of relief organization to help those who will be hardest hit by what's likely to happen. And to help them hang onto what they've got."

When I told him who I had in mind, he took off his glasses and polished them again.

"Why, Allen works for the City."

I said he could quit and go to work for me.

"Maybe. It mightn't be quite that simple. He doesn't strike me as the sort who would jump from one camp to the other. Have you talked to him yet?"

"Not yet. John told me to see you first."

He asked me then what John thought about the chances of getting David.

"Not much," I confessed.

"Well, whoever does the job, you'll be better off to incorporate," he explained, and went on to point out the advantages of a corporation, chiefly that the owner of a corporation could be anonymous.

"We'll file in Los Angeles County, not up here. It won't attract attention."

He said he had a correspondent in Los Angeles who would take care of all the details.

"George Barton would do it for love," he chuckled. "He hates the city administration that much. Nobody will ever know a thing about it. He'll name three of his law clerks as incorporators and they'll endorse the stock in blank, and George will send it to us. You just put the certificates away and forget about 'em. Of course, we'll have to file a certified copy of the articles of incorporation up here in Inyo County." He frowned in anxious thought, then shrugged. "Coming from L.A., I don't think that'll start anybody snooping. . . ." He rubbed his bald head, squinting at the ceiling.

"Let's see, we'll incorporate for twenty-five thousand dollars, twenty-five hundred shares at one hundred dollars each par value. Oh, yes, we've got to have a name. Thought of one?"

"Golden Valley Lands?" I ventured. I had turned over in my mind dozens of names in the sleepless hours of the nights.

Will scribbled on a piece of paper.

"Good enough," he commended. "Might mean anything. Tells nothing." He stroked his nose with the pencil, leaving a smudge. "A darn good name! Let nosy people guess that one. Los Angeles, for instance." He chuckled. "Well, that's about all I need, Abigail. I'll take care of the legal end. All you've got to do is persuade young Allen."

It had been no easy task to take David, step by step, over the long road that began at Minersville and ended that afternoon in our sitting room. But I did it, and in the doing sought to forget nothing that might touch him or mold the future I had in mind for him. As soon as it was over, I knew I had lost. There was no weakening in David Allen's determined, hard-chinned face.

"I'm to take your answer as final?" I asked at last, knowing I sounded forlorn. "You . . . you refuse to accept my offer, David?"

"It isn't a refusal exactly, Mrs. Weston." David looked embarrassed and stubborn and thoroughly unhappy. "It's just that I don't see my way clear to quit what I'm doing. I . . . I don't believe I'd feel right about it."

"Do you feel right about staying where you are?" I couldn't help demanding. "Now you know of all the hardship and sacrifice that's gone into the making of Golden Valley? Knowing what is bound to happen if your city has its way?"

David looked more troubled than ever, but showed no sign of weakening.

"That's just it, Mrs. Weston. I don't know what will happen and I can't understand how you can, frankly."
92

I closed my eyes for a moment. "Have you given any thought to . . . Abby?" I asked. "What will it do to her, with you on one side and she on the other?"

"I haven't thought of very much else," he said quietly.

"Then you don't feel that you owe loyalty to her as much, or even more, than to Los Angeles?" I pressed him relentlessly. He could not know I was trembling all over.

His face flushed. "I don't think quitting my job would be loyalty to her or anybody."

"Who's loyal to whom? And what's this about me?"

In the doorway was Abby and behind her, John.

"What's going on?" Abby came quickly into the room and stood close beside David who had risen to his feet.

"Nothing, Abby," David said quickly. "We were just talking."

"That's not the whole truth, child," I said on an impulse. From the corners of my eyes I saw John move quietly to the fireplace. "I offered David a position, working for me. He refused it."

"Position? Working for you?" Abby turned a bewildered face from David to me. "What are you talking about?"

David's face came up, startled as a fawn's, but I wouldn't stop. It was Abby's right to know what so deeply concerned her, and I meant to make a clean breast of my part in it. I told her about Uncle Amos' gift and what he had charged me to use it for. I told her of my company, Golden Valley Lands.

"There are dark days ahead, Abby," I said, meeting her clear, wide eyes. "It was my thought to use that money to lighten the burden of people who are bound to be hurt.

In a way they are helpless. It will be a long battle and many may go down before it's won. Some of those who will suffer and are too proud to beg I could help with Uncle Amos' gold. I asked David to quit the city and administer the fund. He says he can't do it. That's what we were talking about."

I sat back in my chair and pressed my hands tightly together to conceal their trembling. I could see my little bundle of crocheting on the table, within reach, but I was afraid to attempt it. These days I seemed always to be weeping or quivering or betraying weaknesses I thought I had long since overcome. It was as if I, instead of young Abigail, were in love!

Abby made no answer, and the seconds ran into minutes. John stood quietly watching them both.

"So that's what the loyalty was about," Abby said at last, and her little chin flashed up proudly, but I could have sworn it quivered ever so slightly. "I'm *glad* David said no. He couldn't jump from one side to the other, just like that. But you're a darling just the same, Hanny. Only you can't get it into your dear head that Dave and I have to work this thing out without the help of some sweet fairy godmother—even you!"

She moved over to my chair. The hand she slipped into mine was cold as ice but steady.

"When do you want me to go to work?" she asked simply.

"Work? You?" I echoed stupidly. "What are you talking about?"

"I don't mind being second fiddle. You tried to hire

94

Dave and he turned you down. So I come along at the right moment and you hire me. Simple, isn't it?"

I tried to laugh. "But this is man's work," I protested.

"Oh! Why? Does any man know this valley better than I do? Haven't I grown up in it, with its people, one of them! Don't I know all the ranches and who is square and who isn't? *Can't* I handle this just as well as any man, Grandpa John?"

John looked at her and I have never seen him show such pride. "I guess you could," he said.

Abby flashed a challenging look at David. "Aren't I better for this job than you are?"

David hesitated an instant, shifted his feet, then flung his head up. "I don't doubt it," he said soberly. He turned to me. "Honestly, Mrs. Weston, I think Abby could do what you want done wonderfully well. It's grand for her to have the chance and grand for you to do what you are doing. Some day, perhaps, I can help."

Abby bounded away from my chair and over to the fireplace where she slipped into John's arms with one quick motion. It was a trick she had used since childhood. From this vantage point, she flashed a warning look at David.

"Don't make any mistake, young man. I'm going to make it hot for you and those grasping malefactors you work for!"

Over her head, John's eyes answered the bewildered question of my own. *Give her her head,* they said. *You know the value of good, hard work when the heart's not quiet.*

As though John had taken them, my hands stopped their

95

ridiculous trembling. I reached for my crocheting and began working as though Golden Valley's future rested in the meshes of coarse yarn I was shaping with my little hooked needle.

Then all at once we were all laughing and excitedly planning how Golden Valley Lands could best help those who would need its support.

Chapter 9.

I_T was one of Golden Valley's diamond mornings, a blue sky overhead, the Sierra's crest white with new snow. The threads of willows that marked the streams were drab with the brown of killing frost, and frost whitened the shady spots. The air was sharp and crisply cold, stirred by the winds from far, high places; and though the sun shone brightly, there was slight warmth in it.

As I waited in the buggy in front of the courthouse for John to do an errand, a shabby buckboard rattled into Independence from the north and drew up behind me. The loungers who followed the sun around the square eyed it apathetically, and the group of trusties puttering at the brown lawn and dead flower beds scarcely looked up as a drab little man with a black metal disk clamped over his ear got out of the buckboard and went up the walk to the door. He carried a valise that must have been heavy, for it appeared to weigh him down.

In spite of our doubts of Bushnell, my mind little more than registered this sight, for it was full of other things: my new plan, Abby's amazing step in taking it out of my hands, David Allen, and Abby again. I wondered idly what was keeping John, and forgot Bushnell.

"Well, the lid's off." Frank Masters threw his hat and gauntlets onto my sofa and started to shrug out of his overcoat. His face was set in grim lines.

John looked sharply at him. "What do you mean?"

"Los Angeles has filed deeds on about seventy thousand acres." Frank held his rough hands to the fire. "Few hours ago; while you were over there, matter of fact. Art Rankin told me." Arthur Rankin was our county recorder. "Bushnell filed them. I went over to the courthouse and saw the deeds myself. There's a stack that high." Frank held his hand two feet above the table top.

"All run to the city of Los Angeles. Art totaled the acreage. It's scattered, checkerboarded, from Big Pine to all round Bishop. Hell, they won't have enough water to drink up there."

The shocked look on John's face had ebbed and he said quietly, "You're not surprised, are you?"

"I guess not," Frank admitted reluctantly. "Only I guess I'd been sort of whistling to keep my courage up figuring something would turn up. It did. This. Sure hit me below the belt. You know I got a big stake in this thing."

"We all know that, Frank," John answered sympathetically. "The City was bound to file. It clears the air. They're out in the open now." He looked speculatively at Frank.

98

"Yes," he went on. "I suppose you're spread out pretty thin. I just hope you keep your balance."

"What d'you mean by that?"

"This, Frank. A desperate man takes long chances. You're desperate. I'm just hoping you keep cool."

"If you think I'm going to let L.A. take water out of this valley without a fight, you're crazy as a coot!" Frank flared. "I'll throw lawsuits at 'em till they think it's birdshot. It'll take their whole damn staff to keep up. . . ."

"Yes," John said wearily, "you could do that. You could do a mess of things, go hog-wild. And where'd it get you? You can't sue somebody for what he *might* do. We've got to wait until Los Angeles starts *taking* water."

"And let 'em tie up the whole valley in the meantime?" Frank demanded.

John shook his head. "I don't think they can do that. We'll do all in our power to stop them. But don't forget what Will said. There's no law to prevent a man from selling what's his. Listen, Frank—and you too, Abbie—I'm going to tell you something I've never told anyone." He began to slowly pace the room. "Will and I don't believe we can stop Los Angeles if they're determined to go ahead. They've got too much money and influence."

Frank's jaw dropped.

"All we can do is try to hold them down. To keep people from selling. If they don't get enough water I don't think they'll go ahead. If they do. . . ."

Again John was on the move. Once more my lot was to remain at home and wait for the sound of the buckboard's

wheels; wait for news; wait. Then, when he was at home—
a day and a night, perhaps two—I hadn't the heart to ask
questions. I listened to all he volunteered, and crocheted
until sometimes I wondered what I could do with all the
foolish-looking edgings that emerged from my nervous
fingers.

Most of my news I got from Little John, and there was
little encouragement to be read into his stolid reports by
even the brightest optimist. As the realization of what
actually threatened us valley dwellers spread, a wave of
violence swept the countryside.

Fred Lindstrom, as John had feared, sold his ranch to
Los Angeles. Before the ink was dry upon the deeds, before
Fred had had time to pick up and leave, two of his barns,
forty tons of hay, and six horses were destroyed in a fire
that started in the middle of the night. Fred raged, and
hard-faced men suddenly put in their appearance in
Independence and Big Pine, hanging about the saloons
and street corners, alert and watchful as cats. But they
learned nothing. Our valley people met them with grim
silence.

"I guess that fire didn't hurt anything—except the
horses," Little John observed.

Little John never talked idly. "What do you mean by
that?" I demanded. I felt little sympathy for Fred. In my
mind I could see the fine creek that ran through his ranch,
the green ranches on either side that fed from its seepage.
Fred had sold, and for a high price. Those other ranchers
would go back to the desert.

"I hear the city is going to tear down the buildings on
100

places it buys," Little John said. "Cut down all the trees."

"But why?" I gasped.

He lifted a shoulder. "Maybe they want people to think this was all desert."

There were other fires, mostly in and around Bishop. Up there, night riders—masked, well armed—spread terror in their wake. The Braxton place, one of the finest along Gravel Creek, was swept clean; house, barns, sheds, and hay. There had been nothing furtive about that affair. Mounted men swept into the yard at dusk. They lined Ed Braxton and his family up against a fence and set the torch to everything inflammable. But they did take the horses out, first, and let them go. When the place was blazing furiously, one of the men walked up to Ed and struck him in the face.

"That for you, you low-lifed traitor!" he snarled. They were gone as swiftly as they had come, and neighbors came running to help when it was too late.

Striking here, there, and everywhere, men rode in the night and the red glow of burning barns and stacks lit the sky. In their wake, always too late, raced city automobiles loaded with officers. All they found for their pains was the sight of charred timbers and smoking hay.

John's face grew thinner and bleaker as the tally mounted. It was just this sort of thing he had feared and dreaded.

"Whoever is doing it is making our chances worse every day," he groaned to me. "It may be Harry Brewer—sort of thing that could be his meat. Or the Nunez gang. They're pretty rough customers. Could be both. Young Wilkins,

101

too. Remember him at the meeting, young chap from Bishop? Got rid of his place somehow and is down here. Started drinking like a fish."

"That nice boy?" I sighed, remembering the scared, helpless look of his girl wife.

"It didn't take long for him," John said grimly.

Ray Bowman, our sheriff, drove out to talk to John. "We gotta stop this business," he said. "The city's beginnin' to raise hell with me."

"Stop it then," John advised shortly.

"Yeah, I know." Ray lifted his Stetson and scratched his head. "But I thought maybe seein' as how you're the head of the committee, you. . . ."

"Stop right there, Ray," John said curtly. "Don't mix the committee up with what's been going on."

"You seen them headlines in the L.A. papers?"

"Yes, I've seen them." Who had not?

VIOLENCE IN GOLDEN VALLEY . . . OUTLAWS RIDE IN GOLDEN VALLEY . . . CITY PROPERTY WANTONLY DESTROYED . . . GOVERNOR TO INTERVENE . . . LOCAL AUTHORITIES HELPLESS. . . .

Abby was close to much of this violence. She had opened an office in Independence. Its door bore the legend: Golden Valley Lands. And under it she had added, *Susan Abigail Cabot, Resident Manager.* "It sounds more important," she had explained, "as though the main office might be on Wall Street."

She was boarding with the Bradleys where David went

102

to see her whenever he got a chance; and as he was a city man, he would be marked. Worst of all, Abby was driving all over the countryside, alone. Golden Valley Lands had caused quite a bit of talk, and it had been declared in certain quarters that it was nothing but a cloak for some unknown city activity.

I worried terribly about Abby, almost wishing I had never thought of Golden Valley Lands. Once Little John bluntly informed me that I looked "bad." He gazed stonily at me and added, "You sick, Aunt Abbie?" All the concern neither voice nor look revealed, emerged in the quick, unaccustomed touch of his lean dark hand on my shoulder.

"No, Injun," I said, using my son David's old name for him, a thing I almost never did. "It's Abby," I admitted. "I'm worried about her. A young girl like that mixed up with all this trouble. You know her, Little John. She's got no sense of danger, or caution. . . ."

Little John's dark, meaningless stare seemed to pass through rather than over me.

"Don't fret, Aunt Abbie," he said. "I've hired Harry Lee. He stays with her in the office. He goes with her, too. My people know. They look after her all right."

Harry was a fine steady Indian who had worked for us riding cattle. People said he wasn't afraid of anything on earth and was one of the quickest, best shots in the valley. But there was not complete comfort in the knowledge that Little John had known Abby needed a bodyguard.

I asked her outright to give the whole venture up, making a trip in to her office to do it, but I might as well have saved my strength and time.

"I'm going through with it, Hanny," she said quietly, "and that's all there is to it. By the way, I'm paying myself a hundred and fifty dollars a month and expenses when I'm on the road. Don't look so shocked, darling. A good man is worth his salt." Her little chin went up, obstinately, her eyes slanted brightly into a smile her heart did not share.

I had to take what comfort I could in Harry Lee's sturdy presence in the rear of the office.

"I wish I'd kept my mouth shut that day," David told me wretchedly. "Blabbing off about what a good man for the job she'd make. Lord knows I didn't dream things'd get to this pass. They'll be worse when the construction crews move in."

"If you'd accepted my offer, neither of us would have had all this worry," I retorted.

"I couldn't," he muttered doggedly. "Maybe the time will come when I wish I had."

"We'll try not to take it so hard about Abby," I offered, sorry for my little stab.

"Harry Lee is good," David said. "And Little John and his people. There are a few of us fellows, too. . . ." He flicked his boots with his crop, took a restless turn round the room, and stopped before the window, staring at nothing. "The solution, of course, is for us to get married," he broke out vehemently. "But that's just wishing. Abby won't quit what she's set out to do. I want her to—and yet, I guess I'm all the prouder of her because she hangs on."

As the wave of violence continued and neither our own peace officers nor the special men sent from Los Angeles seemed able to quell it, John, Frank Masters, and Paul Gideon went down to Los Angeles for a conference with city officials. Henry refused to go, declaring he'd "get mad and stay mad" and do more harm than good.

Nothing was accomplished in the end. The city people were polite, but there was a tense undercurrent in all they did and said.

"They don't like what's going on up here," John told me when he got home. "And I don't blame them."

Angus MacAndrew insisted that much of the trouble was because so many good ranches would be ruined when the city actually began to take out water, and that there was no compensation in sight. He fought hard to get his point over, and at one time, John said, he seemed in a fair way of doing it. Then a member of the Water Board—a man called Sayville—stepped in and blocked him.

"He's a mystery man," John told me in exasperation. "He's very wealthy. Said to exert tremendous power in city affairs. You wouldn't like him, Abbie. A long-faced, supercilious ass. Wears glasses on black ribbon. Most of the time he lets 'em dangle, but when he feels like getting extra impressive he fits them on that long nose of his and does his best to stare you down." He scowled.

"This man Bushnell, up here, has been Sayville's jackal for years. Why couldn't Sayville, through his man Bushnell, be responsible for a lot of the dirty work going on up here? It seems to me it'd be a natural play for anybody who wanted to discredit us."

"Why would he want to do that?" I asked.

John shook his head. "I've an idea we'll find out. I

105

broached the notion to MacAndrew. He didn't say much, but I could see it set him to thinking."

The conference ended in a near-quarrel. Driven by Sayville's continued objections and quibblings, MacAndrew lost his temper. "Verra good," he'd shouted. "I hae gi'en my worrd. I'm going to keep it. Think it o'er, an' be no too lang aboot it. Else I'll feel free to go to th' people and tell 'em my story! Ye'll not like that at all, nor will I. But I'm damned if I'm havin' my ditch befouled before the first shovel of dirrt is turned."

"It created quite a commotion," John chuckled. "Half of 'em were trying to pacify MacAndrew, and the other half were assuring us that justice would be done, and all the while this Sayville leaned back in his chair and grinned like a devil."

In the end it was agreed that a committee would come to Golden Valley, and there was much conversation about justice being done.

"It all sounds well," John said dryly. "Only I'm not forgetting Mr. Sayville. Or those hidden tides and currents and unsuspected whirlpools MacAndrew talked about."

Chapter 10.

*A*BBY was finding her good intentions balked at almost every turn. People were stand-offish, even though she knew them to be in desperately straitened circumstances because of the poor crops we had had. Not in twenty years had there been anything like it. A bitter cold winter had been followed by a blazing summer, cloudless and parching.

One autumn afternoon when the air was soft and golden, Abby rode up to my gate and dismounted with a slowness I could not reconcile with the buoyant Abby Cabot of a year ago. She greeted me with an absent-minded kiss and nodded apathetically when I suggested tea.

I went to tell Gim Lee; and when I came back into the sitting room, the girl was hunched in the window-seat, her eyes far away and brooding. I was just debating whether I should ask about David when she announced glumly, "Harry Lee says he'll go with me to look over the Bishop

107

country. Might as well. I'm not doing much good around here."

She swung her leg, impatiently. "I'm stopped. I go to folks I've known since I was so high. They talk freely enough till I mention the city. Then they shut up like clams. No, they don't rightly need help. They're sort of looking for something to happen. Might be any day now; they guess they can worry along. Much obliged just the same." She sighed. "That's all I can get out of them. There are some, I'm sure, who think we're up to some special dirty work of our own."

I made a vague sound of sympathy, and she went on thoughtfully, "I'd give a lot to know what they expect. I'm sure it's not just talk."

Abby was more sober these days than I had ever known her to be. Even her dress had become more sedate and conventional. The divided buckskin skirts, checkered shirts and gay neckerchiefs, the high-heeled boots were laid aside for tailored suits or plain skirts and blouses.

Just as we were finishing our tea, John came in looking so worn and tired that I persuaded him to lie down on the sofa and let me prepare him an iced drink. There was as great a change in John as in Abby. His step seemed to me slower, new lines had etched themselves into his face, he was thinner, and often so preoccupied that I had to repeat a statement several times.

"Sorry, Abbie girl," he would always say, coming out of his preoccupation. "I've got so much on my mind."

This afternoon, he stretched out and closed his eyes; but when I came in with a glass of apricot nectar, Abby was

108

telling him of her discouragement. She sat on the arm of the sofa, a frown between her brows, one of her hands stroking her grandfather's forehead.

John did not seem too much concerned over Abby's reception by the ranchers.

"We're stiff-necked, up here," he said, "and pretty wary of anything that smells of charity. That is, the right sort of folks are. You've had some of the other kind, I guess?"

"Have I!" Abby exclaimed. "At first I was friendly and sympathetic. I got over that. Little John and Harry both tipped me off."

After a little, she slid off the arm of the sofa and stretched her arms above her head. "I've got to run along. Duty calls." She suddenly held her arms lightly to space, curved them a little, and waltzed slowly about the room, her eyes half closed. Her tilted face was dreamy, and regret caught sharply at my heart. Duty! How hard and drab it sounded, and she was so young . . . and in love. . . .

Suddenly, and fiercely, I wanted pleasure for Abby— dancing, and David's arms about her. It made no difference that at her age I had had far more duty than dancing. All the more because of it perhaps, I wanted life to touch Abby kindly.

She drifted to me, kissed me on the cheek, laughed and came out of her dream waltz. " 'Bye, Hanny. See you when I get back. I'd better go home for the night and get re-acquainted with my family. David's having supper with us." I caught her to me, but she laughed again and pulled away to kiss John. She drew her gloves on, shook her head as she had when her hair was loose about her face, though now it was braided demurely about her smooth little head.

When Abby was gone on these trips, it was Little John who assured me she was all right.

"How do you know?" I demanded.

"My people tell me," was all I could get out of him.

Then she was back home again, baffled and raging.

"What do you think that Los Angeles is doing now?" she cried. "They are fluming water out of the creeks they've bought and dumping it into the river. It's rotten! And to think of that old fool MacAndrew sitting in this very room and preaching about waste! Wait till I tell David Allen a few things about his hero!"

I thought she was going to burst into tears. But she bit her lips and looked stormily out a window till she had herself under control.

"Somebody is buying up land, too," she said and turned to John.

"That's nothing new," he said.

Abby shook her head impatiently. "I mean seepage-watered lands. Buying them up for ten or fifteen cents on the dollar."

John gave a little start. "How's that?"

Abby repeated what she had said. "And neither Mr. Fiske nor Harry nor I could find the trail. It leads somewhere, but everybody's so darn sullen. Nobody will talk! I found the same thing up there as down here. People sitting and waiting for something. That's what put me on the trail of this land buying."

She looked darkly at her swinging foot. "I saw some of the buyers. They look like city men."

110

"Los Angeles?"

Abby shrugged. "The sort that might come from any city, really. Too slick to suit me."

John pulled at his lip. "Will should have told me about this."

"He didn't know."

John pulled out his watch and got up. "I guess I'd better be getting up to Bishop," he said, suddenly grim.

"While you're there you'd better inquire about Frank Masters," Abby threw out.

"What about him?"

"He's lending money all over the place." Abby's eyes met John's squarely.

"Hmmm. Guess I'll go into town this afternoon and have a talk with him. I can go up to Bishop in the morning."

"Use my room," Abby offered. "I'm going to stay here with Hanny tonight. We've been neglecting her." She put her arm across the back of my chair. "In town, Grandpa, see if you can find Little John—drat him. He left a note under the office door, dated last night, saying he wanted to see me right away. Very important. Then I couldn't find hide nor hair of him."

Abby and I had that evening together, and having her again made me realize how appallingly I had missed her. With both John and Abby gone so much, the house had become much too big for me, a silent place in which my footsteps echoed hollowly. Henry came from time to time, it is true, and Joan nearly every day; but neither of them filled the void left by John and Abby.

That evening I asked Abby about David.

111

"I haven't seen him since I went to Bishop." Her dull, quiet tone deepened the fear I had been pushing into the back of my mind.

"Child," I faltered, "you don't mean you. . . ."

"No, Hanny," she assured me sadly. "There's nothing wrong between *us*." Her lips quivered. "I love David with every bit of me. He loves me, too. I know that. But there are times when it seems so hopeless. He can't understand why I'm so bitter toward Los Angeles. *I* can't understand how he can *help* seeing the injustice of it. Now comes the fluming off of this water. That's not going to help any." The discouraged droop of her shoulders pierced me with sadness.

"It'll turn out all right, Abby," I heard myself promising with a ring of assurance I knew was spurious. "It's bound to!"

The smile Abby gave me was the sort one gives to a child whose cherished belief one does not wish to destroy, however foolish it may be.

"Is it bound to come right, Hanny?" she asked in a low voice. "I can't help wondering, oftener than I want to."

In the morning Abby seemed to have shaken off her dejection. It was her singing in the bath that wakened me. She came into my room, wet-haired and glowing, the robe wound tight about her lithe body.

Gim Lee brought breakfast to us in my room, and we took our time, dawdling and talking, refilling the coffee cups again and again. But though she spoke freely enough of David and her feeling for him, Abby's spirits did not drop, and she rode away from the ranch a few hours later, smiling and waving to me.

When four days had passed with no word of her, Joe Ramirez, who had gone into town with some freight, brought back a brief note saying that she and Little John would be away for a few days, that I wasn't to worry. There was not a word of where she was going, or why. The next news I had of my granddaughter came from Mark, up from Olancha.

"What's Abby up to?" he asked curiously. "She and Little John and Harry Lee stayed over night with us the other day, headed south. She seemed so chock-full of business that I thought she might have something important on her mind." He chuckled, "I did my best to pump her, but all I got was that she had found out the valley didn't end at Lone Pine, and she was getting acquainted with the rest of it. Little John and Harry just grunted. When Injuns don't want to talk, they don't."

News of Abby was not all Mark brought.

"The city's dickering to buy Cottonwood," he announced. "That's getting kind of close to home."

I thought of the friendly old Spanish ranch house and its fifty-year-old cottonwood trees going back to the desert, as Little John had said all city-acquired property would. There had been many happy times under those great trees whose shade still held the romance of old California.

"Surely Espinoza won't sell," I breathed.

Mark shook his head. "I don't know. The old man doesn't want to, but they've shown him a lot of money, more than he ever saw. You can't expect it to leave him cold. The

113

kids have all gone, except Maria, and she and her mother are nagging at him to go down to the beach. I'm afraid he'll sell out."

"And I suppose it's Bushnell who's talking to him," I said.

"Guess so. The old man said, 'Leetle feller. Deef. Got one of them things in his ear.' That's Bushnell, all right."

Abby returned, as mysterious about her journey as Mark had found her. But she was more like the old Abby, I thought, light-hearted and teasing.

"No, darling," she laughed, when I pressed to know where she had been and what she had been doing. "I can't tell you. It's a surprise." She mischievously mussed my hair. "A six-thousand-dollar surprise, if that'll do you any good!"

"Six thousand dollars?"

"Six thousand simoleons, Hanny, my pet. That's what this surprise cost me." I stared.

"What on earth are you getting at?"

"That's the surprise," she countered sweetly, and refused to say any more about the matter. I talked, however. I talked at length and pointedly. I might as well have talked to the four winds. I tried Little John quite as unsuccessfully.

"Went prospecting," he said and his mouth twisted. "Pretty good prospects down south."

The next day Abby went back to her office and John came home.

"Everything Abby told us is true, and then some," he

announced. "Somebody's buying up seepage lands, cheap. It isn't Los Angeles. We haven't run down who it is. Frank is lending money right and left. I had a pretty straight talk with him, but don't know as it did any good."

My contribution was to tell John about Abby's mysterious talk of a surprise and spending six thousand dollars on it. John looked as blank as I had.

"I don't know how she could spend six thousand dollars down that way," he said. "But if Little John was with her, I've a notion you needn't worry. He makes very few mistakes."

He took the news of Cottonwood's danger more seriously.

"That's bad," he said with a deep sigh. "With what they have already, it gives the city enough water to warrant going ahead. I hoped we could prevent that."

"Perhaps the Espinozas won't sell," I suggested, not too hopefully. But John shook his head gloomily.

"They'll sell." He rubbed a tired hand across his forehead. "And now I've got to get right down to L.A. Hooper —you know, the city's representative in Independence— caught me coming through and said MacAndrew had been burning the wires for me to get down to the city right away. Important. I don't know what's up, but I'd better go tomorrow. I want to see MacAndrew about this Bishop business, anyhow. Somebody is playing him to win. If he does, they stand to cash in."

David came by on his way into town, a very unhappy David. He had been ordered to Cottonwood Creek in charge of three full crews taking water measurements.

115

"I don't want to get that far away from Abby," he complained, kicking at a hassock. "Not with feeling running so high."

I asked him if Los Angeles had actually bought Cottonwood.

"I don't know. I've heard they were dickering for it." He threw me a level look. "Do you know a place called Haiwee?"

I told him I did, and located it for him. I described it was a spring-fed meadow in a deep draw at the far lower end of the valley where the hills drew close together. "Why?" I said.

"I don't know that, either," he answered. "Only there's a rumor that the department is in a terrible turmoil about the place. I thought you might have heard something. Probably doesn't mean a thing. We get a new crop of rumors every day. And that reminds me! Do you know an old fellow around here with a bristly beard?"

"Sounds like George Pringle," I replied, after thought. "Why?"

"Nothing. Only he ran us off Taboose Creek the other day at the point of a sixshooter. Said we were trespassing."

"Likely you were!"

David shook his head. "I don't think we were. But we didn't argue with him. We got." He looked at me a long time, his eyes dark and troubled. "You wouldn't want to try talking Abby into . . . quitting, now, would you?"

"I might *want* to, very much," I observed, "but I don't think I'd bother trying to."

116

"I'm sure *I* wouldn't," he said bitterly, and went on his way.

When John returned from Los Angeles he had a white-faced and defiant Abby with him.

"And now, young lady," he said as soon as he had kissed me and taken off his overcoat, "just tell your grandmother what you told me."

"We've bought Haiwee," Abby spat on, bluntly.

"For heaven's sake!" I gasped. "What in the world for?"

"Because the city has to have a reservoir, and Haiwee is the only place they can put it. Little John took me down and proved it to me, and I'm not sorry a bit because now we've got the city where we want them! And you can fire me if you want to—but you still have Haiwee."

Abby stood very straight and defiant, a spot of bright color on either cheek, her breath coming quickly after the spate of words.

"All right," John said, "I'll go on from there," he added grimly. Suddenly it began to dawn on me that John was not really put out at all. On the contrary, he was bursting with delight at what had happened.

"What does all this mean?" I cried.

"Just what Abby told you," John explained to me. "She and Little John between them have caught the city flat-footed. It must have a reservoir in this valley. Haiwee is the only practicable location for it, and somehow or other that gang overlooked tying it up. Abby and Little John didn't! The city don't like it *at all*. They don't even mind

117

saying so." He glanced at Abby with a twinkle that was rare, these days.

"You're going to have Mr. Angus MacAndrew on your neck pretty quick, young lady."

Abby tilted her chin. "Let him come."

"All right. You've been warned, remember. I wasn't. Nobody told me anything. I went down there like a lamb to its slaughter." He sounded and looked as reproachful as he could.

"You said yourself you didn't ever want to know anything about Golden Valley Lands," Abby reminded him softly.

By some miracle, it seemed that we had checkmated the city. I tried to get the fact fastened firmly in my mind, but I felt a little dizzy.

"Oh, John!" I cried. "Isn't it wonderful?"

"We-ell," John admitted, "it's pretty good, but I don't know whether it's wonderful. . . ."

"Don't be silly," I protested. "Can anything be *more* wonderful than to have beaten Los Angeles?"

"Beaten Los Angeles?" John echoed. "We haven't *beaten* anybody. We've merely taken a trick, that's all."

"But without a reservoir, they can't go on," I insisted, unwilling to relinquish my sense of victory. "They can't even take their big ditch out of the southern end of this valley." My dreams for Abby and David seemed to draw about me once more, but John's voice sent them scuttling back to obscurity.

"They can condemn, and they will. But that'll take time. In the meanwhile we have something to bargain with.

Don't make any mistake, my dear. MacAndrew is mad as a hornet—and so are the rest of them. They'll take the gloves off now, for sure." He looked doubtfully at Abby. "Maybe I'd better make your office my headquarters for a few days," he suggested.

But Abby was all protest at once. "No, Grandpa! This is my party—mine and Little John's. Bring on your MacAndrew and his gang!"

"They'll bring themselves," John promised dryly. "Watch your step, my dear. From here on this is a fight, and no holds barred."

Chapter 11.

As it turned out, I was an uninvited guest when Abby and Angus MacAndrew met.

Whenever I was in Independence, I made Abby's office my headquarters, leaving packages there to be gathered up when I started home, arranging my time so as to have at least a brief visit with her. This afternoon I thought she looked particularly beautiful. The cold and her excitement over the Haiwee triumph had brought a higher color to her cheeks, and her eyes were brighter than I had seen them in a long while.

After she had warmly welcomed me and fussily settled me in the rocker she had brought from the ranch for my use, she perched herself on the edge of her own swivel chair, her heels caught over its spider.

"No sign of MacAndrew yet," she crowed. "But the city people up here eye me as if I was something the cat brought in—including David Allen. He's acting stuffier

120

than anything, Hanny! Pulls the longest face you ever saw and warns me not to take risks."

I could have reminded her that her grandfather John had taken a similar attitude, but decided against it. Instead, I asked if David wasn't still at Cottonwood. Abby shook her head.

"That's all off. He's tabulating field reports here in town. He thinks he's being punished, that someone suspects him of tipping me off about Haiwee. I never heard of such tommyrot, but—oh!" she broke off, pointing to the window.

Two mud-splashed automobiles had pulled up in front of the office. Overcoated and mufflered men climbed out of them, and I recognized MacAndrew's bulk and Mr. Hooper, the city's local representative, but none of the others. The door opened and they came trooping in until the little room was filled to capacity. I had time to see how pinched and cold their faces were and, out of the corner of my eye, to observe that Harry Lee laid his paper down. I moved my chair into the corner near Abby's desk where I would be inconspicuous yet miss nothing.

Abby was on her firmly planted little feet, looking entirely composed. Harry Lee tightened his belt with a casual motion, and introductions began, brusquely performed by MacAndrew.

The names came too fast for me, but I gathered that Abby was being honored by a call from the entire Water Board of the great city of Los Angeles. In addition were engineers, an assistant attorney, and a very unhappy-looking Mr. Hooper.

Abby acknowledged each introduction with perfect

121

dignity, carefully keeping her hands in the pockets of her jacket. Like a charming hostess she invited them all to find seats, and sat down facing them. I looked at MacAndrew, expecting from what John had said that he would open fire. Instead, a rather stout, pleasant-faced man—whose name, it developed, was Hopkins, and who was president of the board—smiled almost benignly and wagged his head.

"Well," he said, too easily, "this is a surprise. I didn't expect to meet so charming a young lady." His gaze swept admiringly over Abby from head to foot, and his beaming exploded into exaggerated laughter as though it were all a great joke.

"I'd like to laugh, too, Mr.—Hopkins?" Abby said, her brows rising delicately, "only I don't see the joke."

"Joke? Ha, ha, ha! Very good indeed." Hopkins' heavy frame shook with laughter, but his little eyes were as cold as marbles. "Perhaps you're right. Perhaps there's no joke at all. Perhaps I'd hoped it might be. You see, my dear young lady"—I saw Abby's eyes narrow—"we've had a neat trick pulled on us, so neat that we think there could be a mistake—somewhere."

"I don't care very much for the word 'trick,' Mr. Hopkins," Abby said, frigidly. "As for there having been a mistake, I hardly think so. But do go ahead."

It was like a play and I was a thrilled spectator, my eyes moving avidly from the face of one actor to another: Abby, composed but uncomfortably alert, Mr. Hopkins, Angus MacAndrew, the others huddled in the shoddy little office. Among them was a lean, slightly too well-dresed man who

122

played with a pair of glasses hung on a black ribbon around his neck. My memory failed me for a second, then recalled John's description and the name. The gentleman must be John Sayville.

The group, in a half circle, faced Abby. At the back of the room, looking blank and missing nothing, was Harry Lee. The tea kettle Abby used to keep the air in the room moist, sang fussily on the ugly iron stove. On the wall was a large map of Golden Valley, and smaller ones showing the different districts. On these were many patches of red, and suddenly I realized that among these was Haiwee. Mr. Hopkins' marble eyes turned toward it, clung for a second, turned back to Abby again.

"Fair enough, fair enough." The man's lush geniality was irritating. Certainly it was not reflected in MacAndrew's smoldering eyes, or on Sayville's cold, aloof face, or in the alert watchfulness of the Attorney.

Before Hopkins could go on, the front door opened silently and Little John came in. Without looking at either Abby or me, he went around behind the grouped chairs and sat down beside Harry Lee. The interruption brought a moment of hush, and all eyes followed the Indian. Then, Hopkins pulled his chair closer.

"Fair enough," he said once again, and all his bluff heartiness had vanished. "So we'll get down to business. You or your company is the owner of Haiwee Ranch—Draw, I think you call it."

"My company," Abby replied briefly.

"Exactly. That's unfortunate for . . . for us." Some of the butteriness had slipped from Hopkins' tone.

123

Abby waited, looking steadily at the heavy face on which a dingy flush was slowly rising.

"I suppose you're aware that Los Angeles must have that particular piece of property?" he asked, his body as still as it had been mobile a few moments before.

"I am." Abby's mouth tightened.

"So you bought it."

"No."

Hopkins seemed taken aback, then he shrugged. "We'll waive examination of motives," he said, as though he intended to be patient, whatever the cost. "The point is that you own the property. We need it. What will you take for this property?"

"It is not for sale," Abby replied quietly.

There was an uneasy stir in the room.

"I suppose you're aware that we can condemn it through the courts?" Hopkins asked with such deadly calm that my heart began to pound. Abby nodded.

"So I have heard. I suggest you begin. I'm told condemnation proceedings are long-drawn-out. . . ."

Hopkins' face took on a mottled hue. Sayville glanced down his nose, and MacAndrew spoke up.

"Let's hae done wi' the sparring," he rumbled. "Ye paid six thousand dollars for yon Haiwee, Miss. I offer ye twenty-five thousand here and now, spot cash and hard money —since that's your pleasure."

He glared at Abby and waited. The room was so still I could hear Abby's breath. Clearly, the city needed Haiwee desperately. And I had been out of patience with Abby for what I had thought was her folly!

"It is not for sale, Mr. MacAndrew," Abby reiterated, quietly.

"Hoot!" MacAndrew snorted. "Onything's for sale—sine the price is high enough. I've made our bid. You mak yours. We're no unreasonable. . . ."

"I've no bid to make, Mr. MacAndrew."

MacAndrew heaved himself up from his chair. "Ye mean ye will na deal?" he demanded, looking slightly apoplectic.

"Yes." From the corner of my eye I saw Harry and Little John standing, their hands hanging loosely at their sides.

"Then, by the Eternal," MacAndrew shouted in a frenzy, "we'll—"

Sayville interrupted with an indeterminate sound. He put his glasses on and studied Abby as though she were a rare specimen that had caught his interest.

"Don't you think, young lady," he said in a pleasant and conversational voice, "that our offer deserves presentation to your principals?"

"It wouldn't do any good," Abby answered, so sweetly that I wondered how she contrived to keep her unruffled composure with all those eyes upon her. "My principals are aged and infirm." I swallowed audibly. "They don't understand business. It only confuses them. . . ."

Sayville's look became one of bored curiosity. "Doubtless you know best. Nevertheless, there are certain factors you might consider at your leisure. There is a great deal at stake in this matter. The welfare of some three hundred thousand people, perhaps thirty million dollars. There are doubtless private investments, too. There are—well, there are so many factors involved that it would not be practical

125

to go into them now. But of this, my dear, be quite assured: neither the city of Los Angeles nor this board is of a mind to be subjected to extortion. Nor are we of a mind to see a great project hindered by petty obstacles. In fact"—he took his glasses off and squinted thoughtfully at them—"we would feel justified in taking very drastic steps."

The stillness of the room grew ominous. Not once had the man raised his voice, but I was filled with a mixture of dread and anger. To this day I do not know how I was so suddenly on my feet and speaking.

"You are threatening my granddaughter," I heard my own voice say sharply, and I sent him as piercing a glance as it was possible for me to muster. He bowed.

"I am aware of that, Mrs. Weston," he answered imperturbably. He rose, a little belatedly, from his chair. He looked about the small office.

"There appears to be nothing to keep us here, gentlemen," he said icily, and started for the door.

There was a scraping of chairs and I saw MacAndrew take a step forward till he was towering over little Abby. Little John and Harry moved in.

"As for ye, Miss," MacAndrew boomed, shaking his finger in Abby's face, "ye've had yere fair chance. From now on this is war. Sine it takes one year or ten we'll have yon Haiwee. In the whilst I'll dig my ditch to its very edge. When th' courts gie the final worrd, I'll droon ye under forrty foot o' water. Come hell or high water, my city drinks. Come on, men!" And he stamped from the room, his men following him.

126

When the door had closed on them, Abby gave a low whistle and sat down, fanning herself.

"You did right," Little John said without expression.

"Your aged and infirm principal agrees," I quavered in a voice that betrayed my earlier anxiety.

But Abby shook her head. Her color had drained away and she looked pinched and small.

"I'm . . . I'm frightened," she said, breathlessly.

"What of?" I demanded. I was just as frightened, but I hoped to keep her from knowing it.

"That man. That Sayville—"

"Rubbish," I retorted, with more bravado than courage.

Little John looked at me and shook his head. "No," he muttered and stared at the blank expanse of the closed office door.

David arrived at the ranch, looking twenty pounds lighter, his eyes red-rimmed and bloodshot.

"There's somebody hanging round the Bradleys' at night," he blurted out.

"How do you know?" My breath felt short. "The Bradleys'" meant one thing to me, now—Abby's boarding place.

"Johnnie Bonham saw him night before last. He made a rush for him but missed whoever it was. The other boys hunted but couldn't find anything."

"Johnnie Bonham? Other boys?" I looked helplessly at David for explanation.

He brushed a hand across his eyes. "I guess I don't make sense. I don't seem able to think straight any more."

He began again, gropingly. "We—I mean us fellows—hear a lot of stories. Most of 'em turn out to be moonshine. A few seem to fit together with what we know."

I sat still, not even looking at him, keeping my eyes fixed on the window and the falling snow that was whitening yard, trees, and shrubs, fearful that I might inadvertently break his trend of thought. I *must* know what he was talking about.

"There's a crowd down in Los Angeles, Mrs. Weston. We don't know who they are. But they've been buying up subirrigated ranches dirt cheap. We talked it over and have figured they're playing MacAndrew for a winner in his fight for that kind of ranch."

I looked away quickly, lest my face betray my thoughts. Angus MacAndrew, champion of the little fellow, and Angus MacAndrew, bullying a slip of a girl, constituted a paradox beyond my powers of acceptance. There would be more about Mr. MacAndrew before we were done.

"They'd cash in big if he wins out," David went on. "We hear they've sunk a lot of money up here. They're likely to be pretty drastic with anything that stands in their way. Abby's getting hold of Haiwee does. It's the only reservoir site there is, Mrs. Weston."

"I understand the city can condemn the property," I said, and waited for his reaction to that.

"That's not the point," he answered readily. "Maybe they can. I don't know. But that could be made to take a long time. Things in courts generally do. In the meantime, this crowd's money would be tied up indefinitely. They aren't going to like that at all, Mrs. Weston."

I looked levelly at David and he did not flinch under my gaze. "I don't know what they can do about it," I said.

"That's just it. Neither do I. But one thing's sure; they'll do *something*. That Abby's a girl and within her rights won't cut any ice with a gang of that kind. She's in their way and they'll put the screws on her."

"Rubbish!" I said, but David Allen must have sensed there was not much force behind the retort. "Things like that don't happen in this day and age," I added.

He gave me a pitying look. "No? You saw J. G. Sayville? We're sure he's in on it. You know Bushnell. He's Sayville's henchman." I recalled with a jolt that John had said that, too. "Those fellows won't stop at anything. That's why a bunch of us got together to take turns watching out for Abby. Now we find somebody else hanging around. That was a nice dish! I went straight to Little John and he looked blank as a stone wall and said not to worry. Not worry!" David gave a bitter laugh.

"Have you said anything to Abby?" I asked.

"No, I haven't." He sighed. "You know Abby. These days she's more independent than ever. It just doesn't get anybody anywhere to let her suspect she needs help of any kind."

"You have complete faith in Mr. MacAndrew, David?" I asked, holding his distracted gaze.

"Absolutely."

Quietly, as objectively as I could, I told him of the happenings in Abby's office. When I had finished the story, he said nothing for a long time, staring at the floor. At

129

last, dully, incredulously, he spoke, not raising his eyes, "He said that to Abby?"

"He did, David."

After another prolonged silence, he got dazedly to his feet. His face was very pale.

"Thank you for telling me, Mrs. Weston," he said lifelessly, still not looking at me. "I'd better be going, now—"

As I watched him walk out of the room, I longed to call him back, to touch his hand, to ask him by word, or look, or touch to forgive me for stripping him of his illusions. But I pressed my lips together and worked my absurd hooked needle in and out of the bits of string.

Chapter 12.

I REDOUBLED my efforts to per-
suade Abby to give up her work and come home. I commanded, argued, and pleaded. But I might as well have
talked to the desert winds. I told her exactly what David
had told me—and I fear I embroidered the facts a little
in my anxiety over her. But she was angry, not worried.

"So that's what he's up to!" she cried. "I thought I heard
something, once or twice. Well, he isn't doing it any more.
He isn't around. He quit his job."

I tried to cover my start. "What's he going to do? Why
did he quit—do you know?"

"No. He just came rushing in the other day and said
he'd quit, that he was going home for a week but would
be back."

From her manner Abby might have been discussing the
weather. Bewildered, I went back to the subject, renewing
my pleadings.

131

"It's my duty to tell your grandfather all about this," I made the mistake of saying.

"I don't care, Hanny," she retorted, her eyes clouded with anger and frustration. "Tell Grampy, too, and Dad and Uncle Mark and Little John—the sheriff, too. Only I'm not quitting."

I knew she would never had used such a tone to me if she had not been nearly beside herself. So I concealed my hurt and hunted out Little John instead.

"I know," he said calmly when I had repeated what David had told me. "They saw Johnnie Fox. I got to learn Johnnie how to keep watch."

"Johnnie Fox?" I exclaimed. "What's he to do with it?" I knew Johnnie—a good Indian boy who worked at odd jobs, mostly around live stock.

"Keeping watch," Little John uttered, briefly. He fixed his gaze on the topmost pinnacle of Mt. Whitney and kept it there.

I tugged at his sleeve. "Little John Weston!" I cried in exasperation. "You tell me at once what you mean. What all this means. . . ."

"Sure." He looked down at me. "My people watch over Abby. Me, Indian Joe, Johnnie Fox, Harry Brown, Billy Shoshone, Louis Black Eagle, Ed Magee." His shoulders moved. "Dave's friends watch, too. Biggest trouble is keeping out of each other's way."

I stared at him, my hand still clutching his sleeve. I knew every one of those boys. They were reliable, they were fighters, they were the best trackers in the valley.

"Then Abby *is* in danger?"

132

Little John looked at me with as near a show of surprise as he was capable of. "Sure. So's Uncle John and Uncle Henry. You. Me. Anybody that gets in the city's way. They play for keeps."

"Little John, you mean Los Angeles would—" My throat closed on the terrors of my thoughts.

"No. Not Los Angeles. Some people down there, maybe."

"Then Abby's *got* to come home."

"She won't." He rested a hand on my shoulder. I know he felt my trembling. "Don't worry, Aunt Abbie. Nothing's going to happen to her." His face flickered in one of his rare smiles. "Might—to those surveyor boys," he added.

I thought he had finished and I tried to get myself together and still my fears. "Dave's quit the city," he said.

"I know," I said weakly, and told him what I had said to David about MacAndrew and the others.

"He told me," Little John said. "It's all right. And you're wrong about MacAndrew. He's all right. He got mad, that's all."

Before I could say anything to that, he asked when John would be home. I told him I didn't know. "Why?" I asked, my head spinning.

"Tell him Joe Pringle is running round with Bushnell," he said.

Joe was George Pringle's only son, a worthless hoodlum if ever there was one. George alone had never been able to see it. "Shore, he's a mite wild," George would chuckle. "So wiz his old man at his age. You got to let a young colt run." Now the young colt was running and in bad company. George Pringle owned Taboose Creek whose seep-

133

age waters fed Henry's ranch, and Tom Ellison's, the Schultzes', and the McNairs'.

When John came home I took all my troubles to him in one basket: Abby, David, Joe Pringle. John heard me out, then took the problems up in what he considered the order of their importance.

"So the lad's quit, eh? That's all right." His eyes twinkled. "Maybe you did help him along a bit. It wouldn't mean a wedding soon, would it?"

"I wish to goodness it would," I sighed. "That might settle all this nonsense Abby's got in her head. . . ."

But John didn't agree. "I don't think so," he said. "Abby won't quit until she thinks her job's done. Remember the fight that young one put up even to get into this world at all? It's not likely she'll ever lose that spirit. Don't worry about Abby, though. There'll be no breaking through that gang of watchdogs!" He laughed and my spirits lifted to hear him.

"So Little John wanted you to tell me that Joe Pringle's running with Bushnell. That means something, I don't know what. Little John wouldn't have mentioned it if it hadn't been significant." He stretched and yawned. "Don't get excited," he said, "but the city is filing suit to condemn Haiwee. They've got to file up here, but they're going to try awfully hard to get a change of venue down to Los Angeles County. Will says Charlie Hunter won't allow that, but he thinks he'll have to send it somewhere else."

Charlie Hunter was our Superior Court judge, and the thought of him cheered me still further. I went to bed and

134

slept better than I had for a week. But the very next morning I had a second shock. Abby dashed in, her face like a thundercloud.

"I'm through with David Allen," she announced, and I could see tears trembling behind her anger.

"For heaven's sake, what's happened now?" I asked, sinking into my chair with the feeling that I would need support for this new ordeal.

"He—he won't m-marry me. He's the m-most pig-headed. . . ." Abby began to cry, not hiding her face, the tears crawling, unchecked, down her face.

"Child, child," I murmured, drawing her down to me. "Tell me what's happened?"

"He's just pig-headed, I tell you. N-now that he's quit the city we could get m-married—and he w-won't. I hate him, and I could die. . . ." She dropped to her knees, putting her face in my lap.

"There, there, darling." I stroked her soft hair. "Tell Hanny all about it."

"He won't marry me because he's a poor, penniless surveyor without a job," Abby sobbed into my dress. "That's what he says. And I'm a gil-gilded child of great w-wealth and he isn't going to m-marry any woman until he can support her as she's accustomed to being s-supported." Her face popped out of the folds of my dress, then buried itself again. "And I'm free to seek my h-happiness—and he's going away b-but he'll always be thinking of me. Oh, Hanny, what a fool he is—" Her recital ended on a long wail. I closed my hands about her shaking shoulders.

"I'm complimented that you've seen fit to take your aged

135

and infirm principal into your confidence," I said gently, after having let her cry for a while. "But I confess she is badly confused."

Abby straightened herself and settled on the arm of my chair after her long habit, mopping at her face. Her handkerchief was a damp string and her face was spotted with weeping. But she went at composing herself with such determination that I thought the worst must be over.

"There's just no need of his acting this way, Hanny," she said bitterly. "*Is* there?"

"I'm not so sure of that," I ventured cautiously, still stroking her hair. "I'm rather inclined to think he's showing what fine stuff there is in him."

"Fine stuff, nothing!" Abby choked. "Well, he isn't going to get away with it."

"Love seems to get away with a good many things," I suggested.

"Not with me it doesn't," she muttered. Then she threw her arms about me, without warning, and kissed me. I was certain she had not talked it all out of her system, and would have tried to draw her out, but she jumped up and, patting the sides of her hair lightly, ran out of the room. In a moment I heard her horse's hoofs in the road going toward home.

I was still sitting there, turning over in my mind all Abby had told me, when David Allen walked in. As soon as I saw his glum and troubled face, I realized I had half expected him.

"I suppose Abby's told you about us," he said bluntly.

"What about you?" I asked, looking at his bowed head.

136

He walked back and forth across the room a time or two, then came to a resolute stop in front of me.

"She's sore because I say we can't be married. I still say that! Can't say anything else. I've got no job even. I haven't anything. I'm going to open a surveying office up here, but I don't know how it'll work out. Until I find out I can't even think about getting married. But Abby claims that now I've quit the city, everything's all right and I've only to hold out my arms and she'll walk into them. We've quarreled and fought—and got exactly nowhere."

I realized with a pang that all my years and experience counted for nothing against the crisis which belonged to youth and which youth itself must settle. I ached to help, but distrusted what might so easily seem only an old woman's meddling.

"I suppose you gave up your city job because of what I told you?" I said.

"Yes, ma'am," he admitted dully. "Partly anyway." He stared moodily at the fire.

"I went right down to Mr. Mac, and told him straight," David said presently. "He didn't say much. Couldn't expect him to beg me to stay on. But I knew he felt bad. Not only about me—more, I think, about Abby. He just said, 'You know best, lad.' or something like that. 'It's sore hard for a man to see his dreams knocked silly.'"

By the time John came home I felt near to tears myself. I went through David's unhappy recital as exactly as I could recall it for John's benefit.

"Good boy!" he exclaimed. "I knew he had it in him.

137

They'll come out all right." He narrowed his eyes. "A good surveyor might do very well up here—"

His reaction put me in better spirits. If John could see so much hope in this new turn of affairs, it must not be as bad as I had feared. "Something ails a pretty woman if she can't cry now and then," John had teased, and I tried to push the memories of Abby's tears out of my thoughts and take John's brighter view of her future.

The courtroom was full, every seat taken, and behind the seats the space was crowded with standing men and women. They were the same kind of people who had crowded the meeting hall at Independence and the halls at Bishop and Big Pine. They had come from all over the valley—from lonely ranches, struggling homesteads, mines, and prospect holes. The men's faces were weather-beaten and tense with anxiety; the women's shoddy garments showed the same pathetic attempt at adornment, their patient arms held fretting infants.

I could have wept as I looked about, as I had at Independence. I felt a futile rage toward this additional worry and fear inflicted upon people who asked only to be left alone to battle their way ahead as all of us had done.

City lawyers and officials were crowded inside the railing. I saw MacAndrew, older-looking than when he had entertained us in our sitting room, and much more somber. I thought Will Fiske looked woefully outnumbered at his place at the lawyers' table. But the stack of law books in front of him was formidable.

138

The meeting opened with scarcely any preliminary discussion. The city's lawyers were foot, horse, and guns for a change of venue to Los Angeles County. The arguments were too technical for me to grasp, but Charlie Hunter listened carefully, interrupting with a question here, a suggestion there. When the last speaker had his say, Charlie toyed with a pencil, looked over his glasses at Will.

"The Court will now hear arguments in opposition," he announced.

Will spoke briefly, pointing out that the city of Los Angeles was as much a party to the lawsuit as Golden Valley Lands, the defendant, and that if the case could not be tried without bias in Inyo County it most certainly could not in Los Angeles.

"Your Honor," he concluded, and I thought I caught a glint of mischief in his brownie-like face, "I have here citations, but to read them would greatly prolong this hearing. Therefore, if it please the Court, I respectfully suggest that counsel file briefs."

No sooner had he sat down than the whole array of city lawyers were on their feet in protest. They wanted the matter heard and determined here and now. Delay would mean great cost and hardship. The point was simple enough. The Court could determine it in five minutes. And so on, and on. . . .

Will had previously declared to John that time was our greatest need. I knew he was fighting for time, now.

The city Attorney spoke with a gravity that did the occasion justice.

"The Court realizes how vital the issue is, surely," he

said solemnly. "The future of a great city and its people is at stake. Even the President of the United States has declared this to be a case involving the benefit of the many against the few."

How often we were destined to hear that!

Judge Hunter listened intently to all that was said, then considered in a long-drawn-out silence what he had heard.

"Motion taken under advisement," he said so suddenly and crisply that I jumped. "Sixty days to proponent to file opening memorandum of authorities. Thirty days to contestant for reply. Thirty days to proponent for rebuttal. Court is adjourned."

He rapped with his gavel and stepped down from the bench to enter his chambers.

One hundred and twenty days. Four months. Anything might happen in that length of time. There was an audible gasp from the city lawyers, whispering and angry looks. Will was smiling benignly as he gathered up his law books. I had a sudden overwhelming suspicion that these weighty tomes might not, after all, contain so much law on the matter under discussion.

Outside the courthouse, Will chuckled as we all stood together on the sidewalk.

"Charlie Hunter is shooting the works," he said. "Four months before he even has to think about it. Ninety days more before he has to render a decision. Not even then if he doesn't mind not collecting his salary. That's a mad bunch." He jerked his head toward the city men getting into their automobiles.

"What will the decision be?" I asked.

140

Will looked guileless. "I don't know. It's unethical for a lawyer to discuss a case with the judge. Between us, the city is dead right. This case can't be tried up here. Actually, everybody in the valley is a defendant." He looked up at the thin blue Inyo sky. "He might send it over to Mariposa County," he murmured innocently. "He and Judge Meredino are good friends. Both parties would get a square deal over there. The city wouldn't like it much."

I realized that Will Fiske knew exactly what Judge Hunter was going to do.

Little John looked at John, then deliberately rolled and lighted a cigarette.

"The city has bought the Pringle Ranch," he announced.

"What are you talking about?" John's voice was harsh and rasping. "Old George would never sell."

"He didn't. But young Joe did."

"Damn it, Little John, talk sense. How could Joe Pringle sell the old man's place?"

"He didn't. He sold his own place. The old man gave it to him. Joe sold it to Bushnell, last night."

John sat motionless. "How do you know all this?" he asked at last.

"I heard them. Saw Bushnell give him the money. Saw Joe give Bushnell the deeds. One from his father to him, one from him to the city."

"How did that come about?"

Little John raised a shoulder. "There was an empty room next to Bushnell's. He forgot, I guess. It came in handy for me."

John still sat motionless, staring at Little John. In those few minutes his face seemed more weary than I had ever seen it. He stood up, stiffly.

"We better go over and see George," he said tonelessly. "We'll pick up Henry on the way."

When they had gone and I was alone in the silent house, I went back in memory to the first time I had heard of Taboose Creek. Mrs. Wagnall, my neighbor, had described its beauties to me and I had listened with a great longing in my heart. If what Little John had told us was true—and I had no doubt that it was true—Taboose Creek that cut through the very heart of Manzanar was lost forever.

I had only to see John's face, when he returned, to know what I had known all along—that Little John had made no mistake.

"It's all true," John said grimly. "Old George deeded the place to Joe to get out of lawyers' fees and this new inheritance tax. He wasn't to record the deed until the old man died.

"George wouldn't believe it at first. Then he called Joe in. At first, the young whelp denied it. But after Little John went over what he'd heard and seen the night before, he broke down and started sniveling like the cur he is. That's when we left. It's not a pretty sight to see a son who's betrayed his father. The last thing, old George told us not to worry. Said he'd straighten it all out tomorrow morning, maybe."

George Pringle never straightened anything out. In the middle of the night we were awakened by the Indian death wail. "Aiiiiiiiiiiieeeeeeeeeeee!" It shrilled through the night,

142

beating against the sky, seeming to fill the universe with an eerie sorrow. In the morning, Indian Mary told us. George Pringle was dead, stricken in the night in the house he had so proudly built with his own hands by Taboose Creek.

Chapter 13.

*Mac*ANDREW'S Ditch that was to rob us of our snow-fed waters, taking them from the brightness of sky and sun to the gloom of iron pipes under the streets of Los Angeles, crawled inexorably southward.

"Come hell or high water, my city drinks!" MacAndrew had stormed at Abby. It had not drunk yet, but each day the ditch crawled forward, bringing near that time when it would have its water. Only the magnitude of the task itself and Haiwee stood between. We who had been so certain when Abby bought Haiwee that the city's need of it for a reservoir site could be used as a club to bring decent justice to those who saw their ranches dying, began to lose some of our certainty.

Will Fiske came back from the first trial of the city's lawsuit to condemn Haiwee. Charlie Hunter had sent it over to Mariposa County, as Will had foretold. Now even he was dubious.

"I dunno," he observed gloomily. "Meredino did all he

144

could. The record's so full of holes the case is bound to be sent back for retrial. I'm beginning to wonder if the city can't afford time better than we can. They didn't appear in any compromising frame of mind to me."

Frank Masters' bank was forced to close its doors. Disregarding all warnings Frank had gone his stubborn way, trying to fight Los Angeles with dollars—the city that had a hundred thousand dollars to his one. When Frank went down, with him went ranchers, merchants, homesteaders, prospectors, stockmen, and miners. That Frank could not survive the crash of the house he had built, passing away in his sleep before the audit was even begun, didn't shorten the line of those who waited before the doors that would never open again. I saw that line in my dreams again and again—toil-bent men, faded women. Even the children, clinging to their mother's skirts, were strangely silent, their little faces scared and defeated. I avoided that corner of the town as much as I could. The sheriff boarded up the windows and doors after someone had thrown a rock through the plate glass in which Frank had taken such pride.

Day after day tragedy stalked the valley. A Bishop rancher hanged himself in his barn. A Big Pine woman ate arsenic. Another rancher blew the top of his head off with a shotgun. A homesteader from Eight Mile shot himself beside his last dwindling haystack. Jane Calkins moved away from her dying ranch and all she had worked so hard to gain. I heard that she was cooking in someone's kitchen in Pasadena and had been obliged to put her children in a foundlings' home. I wrote to her but never got a reply to

145

my sorrowful, inadequate letter. A young couple in Bishop were found dead in bed, clasped in each other's arms. The coroner's cold, impersonal report was the single word: strychnine.

"City's sore as hell," Little John grunted. "About the Haiwee business. Hear they're going to turn the valley back to the desert."

"But they can't! They wouldn't!" I cried.

Little John looked at me. "Tomorrow," he said, "I'll show you something."

We rode out to Fred Lindstrom's old place. With a sick heart, I looked about me. The meadow was already brown and dead. Wind rattled through the dying orchard and sent the leaves from the old cottonwoods scurrying over the ground. When it caught up a bit of dry ash from where the burnt barn had stood and sent it swirling, I made Little John take me away. I shut my eyes against the weed-grown garden and the empty house with its staring windows.

Fred had been one of the first to sell to Los Angeles. His barns and haystacks were the first to be burned. Fred was angry when he moved to Long Beach. But presently letters began to come from him. In his cramped, Old World handwriting, he begged for news of his mountains, of the valley, of his beloved ranch. Then the letters stopped, and we heard Fred had died of a heart attack. But I knew they had broken his heart.

After Frank Masters' bank failed, ranch after ranch passed swiftly into the city's hands. No longer were the dazzling prices paid. "Take it or leave it," was the city's motto. Penniless people took it, choking back unspeakable heartache. For the others, those with the seepage-fed ranches, there was nothing to do but watch the browns spread and spread, or take the pittance city land sharks offered.

David opened a surveying office. How he managed I do not know. John said he got some work, but to him the important thing, I knew, was to be in the valley where Abby was. I knew they had made up their quarrel, though Abby had not confided in me. They were often together, but there was scarcely a trace of the old radiance.

One day they came over together to see John and me, and Abby's eyes were starry, and David's thin face, flushed and eager.

"You tell her, Dave," Abby commanded, and one question leaped into my mind; but she added, "You thought it all up yourself."

A little hesitantly, David suggested that what was left of Uncle Amos' fund could be put to no better use than aiding the truly needy.

"People are going hungry, Mrs. Weston," he said earnestly. "And they're too proud to beg. Why not forget about notes and security and all the businesslike way of doing things, and get the rest of that money working where it'll do the most good?"

"You'd only dribble it away," John objected, looking curiously at him.

"Maybe so, sir," David's jaw set stubbornly. "But we'd keep them eating as long as it lasted. And that might be long enough. I kind of think the . . . the old gentleman who left the money would like that."

John's tired eyes glowed, and he made no further effort to conceal his pleasure in David. "I kind of think he would like it, too," he said warmly. "Go to it, boy."

"It would only go where it's really needed," Abby put in. "David and I'd be working together on it, you see. We won't get fooled. I know everybody too well, now."

They stood before me, their youth and good will shining in their faces, and my throat filled with a warm ache. I pulled David down to me, kissing him because I did not dare trust my voice to answer.

It was not very long after that before David paid me another visit, this time alone.

"We've got to get Abby out of this mess," he exclaimed. "It's getting awful. The valley's full of riffraff. There are a dozen fights a night, some of them plenty tough. Worst of all, we've found that we're bucking the city cliques. They'd rather the people *wouldn't* eat; they'll break and sell out quicker if they've got empty stomachs!"

I reminded him of Little John's and Harry Lee's faithfulness in watching over Abby. But my reassurance sounded hollow enough, and before I could check the impulse, I asked him if he really loved Abby. He looked at me with a start.

"You know that, Mrs. Weston."

"But you still have your little differences? Even now you're working side by side?"

He nodded. "Some of our—differences, as you put it, aren't so devilish little," he confessed. "Yesterday, for

148

instance, I begged her to get out and leave it to me. We. . . . Well, we had quite a hot battle before it was over."

"Battles will leave scars, David."

"I know. I get so worried about her, I guess I go clean off balance sometimes." He sighed.

"Now there's a sort of truce between us," he went on, unhappily. "*It* doesn't work a hundred percent, either. We never talk about ourselves, but we see each other almost every day. Four or five nights a week, if she's home, I go over to the Bradleys'—but so do other fellows! Little John's always there, sitting in a corner saying nothing. Abby plays the piano and I tinker around with the mandolin. We sing and play crazy games—and pretend we're having a good time." He stared moodily at the floor.

"Time comes to say goodnight and come home, and the bottom drops out of everything. It's upside down. I ought to be coming home to her, not leaving." He fell silent and suddenly got up and put on his coat.

He went without saying goodbye, and I watched from the window as he slung his lean body easily into the saddle and set off down the road.

John was on the go, day and night, good weather and bad. We had a spell of cold, some snow and icy mist, and John caught a chill. He came in, blue-lipped and chattering, and I had Gim Lee rushing for the brandy while I filled the hotwater bottle.

"You're not as young as you were," I scolded when I had him safely in bed.

149

"I'm young enough," John retorted over the rim of his glass. "There's too much to be done to be scared indoors by a spitting of snow."

I could not deny that. The closing of Frank Masters' bank had filled the whole valley with panic. John's quiet voice and manner had a good effect on the frightened people. I have often wondered if anyone ever gauged the true value of those quiet handclasps, the unalarmed, encouraging voice, the steadfast look of John Weston. No one knew, as I did, the great store of comfort that was mine to draw upon, but in some measure it was shared by many in Inyo those dark days.

Though he insisted on getting up and out next day, John's cold hung on, fastening deep in his chest. We had recently bought a fine, modern automobile—a Cadillac, and Little John drove it for John. It did shorten distances, though it did not always run and scarcely a trip was without a punctured tire. After one trip through abominable weather, Little John took me aside.

"You ought to put him to bed, Aunt Abbie," he said. "This is pogonip weather."

It was in the middle of that same night that John wakened me, complaining that he was "burning up." I took one look at his flushed face and heavy eyes and set Joe Ramirez galloping to Independence to get Dr. Morgan at once.

A gray, dismal dawn was breaking as George Morgan finished his examination.

"John's a sick man, Abigail," he said, rubbing his chin. "This city business has drained him to a pulp. Keep him
150

quiet till this inflammation's gone. Even then there'd better be no more of this tearing all over the country in any weather."

He promised to lay down the law to John himself as soon as he was a little better. He did—and so did I. But in spite of our warnings, in a few days John was up, almost too weak to walk. As soon as he had the strength, he was attending meetings again, journeying to Los Angeles. And, as George Morgan had predicted, he soon had a relapse. Henry took over John's work as best he could, while Joan moved in to help me.

A stretch of good weather came, and the sky was clean-washed and high behind the Sierra. I came in, one morning, to find John staring out the window.

"You've been worrying too much about me, Abbie girl," he said. "I'm not near dead yet." I dropped down on my knees beside the bed, and he stroked my hands as he talked. "I've had to do what I've done. We're at a most critical time, Abbie. We thought Haiwee would bring the city to terms before this, but it hasn't. What with that and Frank Masters going to pieces, folks are scared out of their senses—and you can't blame 'em. They've kept lined up pretty well, at that."

When he had rested a little, John went on to explain that injunctions and damage suits were filed every time the city drained a stream, and he and Will always carefully studied the strategy of who should bring suit and when.

"I'm not going to be a damn fool, Abbie," John promised. "I'll slow down. But I can't just hang around home, loafing." He stirred restlessly, and I saw that the flush was rising

151

again in his gaunt cheeks. "Maybe this is a good time to straighten out a couple of things. There are two kinds of city people, Abbie. The honest ones, doing their work sincerely, like MacAndrew—"

I interrupted with a scornful sniff. "They can have their Mr. MacAndrew."

"I know," John smiled. "When it comes to Los Angeles, you figure the only good Injun is a dead one. That's partly right. But not all the way. I happen to know MacAndrew has worked like the devil for the seepage ranches. I know the work of his Ditch is honest. I'm convinced he never had a hand in that skulduggery in the beginning. Los Angeles needed water, and he saw enough up here, he thought, for all. From that point on he went to work planning how to carry it to his city, leaving the acquiring of it to others. That's where the vultures came in. They're still around, picking every loose dollar they can see. They're the ones we've got to lick—and Haiwee is our ace in the hole."

"What about the seepage ranches that are being ruined?" I demanded.

"That's who we're fighting for, and MacAndrew too, Abbie. It's because of him that I can't sit back and twiddle my thumbs."

Little John was in the kitchen, sipping a cup of coffee, when I went downstairs.

"Something's hatching," he said. "I don't know—yet."

"What makes you think so?" I asked.

"Those fellows have quit talking."

"What fellows?"

"Oh, Wilkins, Brewer, the Nunez boys, Rawlins. . . ."

"Rawlins?" I had never heard the name before. Little John's eyes flicked sharply.

"Bird dog for Bushnell, I think," he grunted. "Some city powder's missing. They say us valley people stole it. I think Bushnell and Rawlins did. I'll find out."

"What difference does that make?" I asked querulously.

Little John gave me a long look.

"Maybe they'll blow up the Ditch," he speculated. "Maybe they could stir up Brewer and that crowd to do it. They could use city powder and say we stole it. There's lots of things they could do. All of 'em bad."

"They wouldn't dare," I breathed, feeling sick.

"There are city people with money tied up here. They figure on cleaning up." He laughed shortly. "They'd do anything. But don't tell Uncle John. Get him well quick. He's the one the crooks and the Brewer outfit are most afraid of."

Chapter 14.

*T*HE weather did not improve. We had rain—snow, rain, sleet, rain again. That Sunday came in overcast, sullen gray clouds piling over the mountains and spreading across the valley. By mid-morning the first flakes fell, and soon the countryside was veiled in white.

John seemed much better and very cheerful, almost welcoming the snow.

"That'll keep me in better than you and George Morgan," he laughed, swinging himself out of bed. "I'm going downstairs. I'm tired of this. Besides, Gim Lee will have chicken and dumplings, or I'm a Dutchman. I never will get used to eating in bed."

When we sat down to our midday dinner, John's spirits were so high that mine soared also, but by three he was weary again, his eyes grown heavy.

"Get sort of petered out, this time of day," he admitted as I tucked him into his freshly tidied bed. "Guess I'll nap a little. . . ." As I drew the curtain and opened the window a crack, I saw that he had already dropped into a doze.

As the early winter dusk closed in, the uneasiness that had hung over me all day increased. I wandered into the big, bright kitchen, finding comfort in its warmth and lightness. There was no wind, only from time to time the thump of snow, falling from the trees to the roof. Then, in the hushed silence of the falling snow, I heard the sound of wheels and the laboring of a hard-driven team.

I caught up a lamp and ran to the door, my hand between the chimney and the draft. Though I could see nothing through the dense curtain of snow, I recognized David Allen's voice, and before I could find my own to call out, Abby's slim figure emerged from the shifting wall of white.

"Hanny," she cried, "Oh, Hanny!"

I could feel her trembling as she clung to me, and then David loomed out of the darkness into the circle of light. Putting my finger to my lips, I pushed them into the kitchen, closing the door as softly as I could.

"Don't wake your grandfather," I cautioned, setting the lamp on the scrubbed white wood of the big table. "What is it?" I whispered, as water dripped from Abby and David to form puddles on Gim Lee's shining floor.

"They're blowing up the Ditch tonight," David said breathlessly. "The Rawlins, Wilkins, Nunez crowd."

I knew what John thought of the men who bore these names and to what lengths they were capable of going.

"Where?" I gasped.

"At the north end of the Alabama Hills. Little. . . ." David stopped abruptly.

"A very good place, too." It was John's voice. I whirled about to see him standing at the door in robe and slippers. One hand rested against the door frame. "That'll make a big show—won't be hard to fix. If I were doing it I think I'd pick some place else." I saw him sway a little.

"John!" I cried. "Please! You must go back to bed!" I rushed to him, and he took my hands, pushing me away, gently and absently, as if his mind were on other things.

"All right, Dave," he said, going over to a chair near the stove. He sat down and took a deep breath. "What's the story?"

I had followed John halfway to his chair, then stopped because of the violent trembling of my knees. Abby had her arm about me, but she too was trembling.

"Little John came over to the Bradleys'," David was explaining. "He got us outside and said he'd found out they were going to blow up the Ditch tonight. Said for us to get out here and tell you, that you'd know what to do. I didn't mean for you to hear, though—I knew you weren't up to—ought not to have bothered, sir. . . ."

John passed a hand over his face and I saw the veins standing out dark against the pale flesh. "Little John," he said. "That means it's all true enough. Yes, I know what to do about it."

"I'll go over and get Mr. Cabot," David offered nervously. "The team's outside. We'll go see what we can do. Any suggestions, sir?"

156

John looked up at David, and the drawn, darkened corners of his eyes wrinkled in a smile.

"Tell Henry to dress for horseback. Get him back here in a hurry. Rout out Joe at the bunkhouse. Tell him to saddle Lo, Pete, and Prince. I'll be ready by the time you get back. Come upstairs, Abbie, and help me get dressed." He stood up.

All the concern I had felt for the plight of my neighbors deserted me in a rush of panic. Nothing mattered but this sick man before me. I flung myself at him.

"Let them blow up everything!" I cried. "You mustn't go out. You can't! I won't let you. Please, John, please—please—"

As he had at the door, so now he again took my hands gently in his. But now he did not push me away from him. He held my hands tightly.

"Take it easy, Abbie girl," he said smiling into my terror-smitten face. "I'm all right. I've been out in worse weather than this. It's just two-three miles over there. I'm the only one who can handle this. Come on." He took me by the arm and moved toward the door. "Get going, Dave. We haven't much time."

David did not move. His face was stubborn, his eyes moved from Abby to me, though he spoke to John.

"You can't go out tonight, sir," he said. "It's bad. It might be the death of you. Just give me a hint or two and Mr. Cabot and I can take care of everything. Just tell me—"

"You'd likely get yourselves taken care of," John said grimly. He looked at David and his face hardened. "You do what I tell you—and quick. Dave, this is no time for

157

damn' foolishness. Come on, Abbie." His hand tightened on my arm and he started again for the door. David hesitated a moment, then strode from the kitchen and the door slammed behind him, the window curtains stirring in the cold breath that eddied through the room.

Upstairs, even as I gathered his warmest clothes together, I kept begging John not to go. Tears blinded me, and I made no effort to hide them. White-faced and silent, Abby helped me. When he was almost dressed, John kissed me tenderly.

"Listen, both of you," he said firmly. "Try to understand how critical this thing is. I think I'm the only one who may be able to stop this business. If they pull it off, I don't know what the end might be. It will ruin every ghost of a chance we've got. It surely is worth taking some risks to prevent. I'm better and you know it. Look at me—bundled like a mummy." He looked down at his grotesque bulk. "Nothing's going to happen to me. Stop worrying. Get my spurs, Abby, like a good girl."

She was just buckling them on when Henry burst into the room, his face black and forbidding.

"John, you damn' fool, get into your bed," he shouted. "You don't think you're going anywhere, do you?" He whirled on poor Abby. "Have you and Dave got the sense you were born with—coming out here with this? Where is Little John?"

"I don't know." Abby's voice was toneless, her face a white mask. "He just vanished. Said he had something to take care of."

"Humph! I guess he must have!"
158

"Oh, shut up, Henry," John said wearily. "The kids did right. And you know I'm going over there. So why waste time and breath carrying on about it?"

Silenced, Henry went with the rest of us down to the kitchen. Somewhere David had found chaps and a pea-jacket. Abby had gone downstairs before us and was with him.

John looked approvingly at David, then turned to me. "Keep a fire going, Abbie, and a pot of coffee. We'll want some warming when we get back." He looked sharply at Henry. "Neither of you boys heeled?"

Henry shook his head and David muttered, "Nope." John put his arm about me, drawing me close.

"Now, no worrying, girl," he said, and kissed me. "Before you know it we'll be back wagging our tails behind us."

The door shut behind them, seeming to close on my heart, and Abby and I were left to that hardest of all woman's tasks—waiting. I sank into the nearest chair and gave way to sobs. Abby let me cry till the worst of the storm was over, then dropped to her knees beside me and pressed her cheek against my wet one.

Seconds ticked into minutes and the minutes dragged somehow into hours. Gim Lee appeared and perched upon his stool, his parchment face expressionless. Abby tried to make talk, but her voice choked into silence usually before a sentence was finished. I started to make some coffee, but Gim Lee snatched the pot from my hands.

"Woman coffee no good," he sing-songed. "Me makee strong likee hellee. Sit down!"

Abby found a deck of cards and began to play solitaire.

159

Gim Lee thrust a cup of scalding coffee at me, but though I lifted the cup to my lips at intervals, I could not drink. I looked at the clock and saw with a sinking heart that only one hour had gone by. They could not have reached the place yet.

"Sonabitchee!" Gim Lee crashed a pot upon the stove and began to fill it with water.

"Now, Gim Lee—" I faltered my protest so feebly it had no effect. He repeated his epithet and set another pot on the stove.

"Let him alone, Hanny," Abby said huskily, and I saw her chin was quivering.

I went to the door, straining my ears for the hoofbeats I knew I could not hear. Abby, who had been sitting on the floor, stood up and gently forced me back into my chair. She began to talk of the work she and David had been doing, and I tried to listen, but my mind was no more on what she was saying than hers was.

The hours dragged on. Abby sat quiet, stroking my hand. Gim Lee perched on his stool, brooding and sullen. It was a little past midnight when I heard a horse snorting, the jingle of spur chains, and the squeak of saddle leather.

I reached for the lamp, but Abby caught it up from the table before I could touch it, and Gim Lee noiselessly swung the door open. A square of yellow light flowed from the lamp into the slanting snow.

"Easy," we heard Henry's voice in warning. "Easy down with him, Davy. Whoa, there! Stand still!"

I plunged into the night, stumbling through the drifted snow, every nerve straining toward the bundled, snow-

160

powdered figure that Henry and David were lifting out of the saddle. My hands found and touched it, my arms went instinctively about it. Together we got him up the steps and into the warmth of the big kitchen. My hands fought and won, pushing the others away. None but my hands should untie the muffler, remove the sodden overcoat, unbuckle the straps, pull off the boots, fumbling but frantically fast. John's eyes were half closed, his breath labored and audible.

"Is he shot?" I heard myself whispering over and over like a maniac.

"No," Henry whispered back. "Collapse. Let's have some whisky."

Abby flew to the cupboard, but Gim Lee was ahead of her. I snatched the bottle from him, spilling some. A little of the burning liquor trickled down John's throat. He strangled and his limp body shuddered feebly against mine. Henry tilted the bottle to his own lips and drank deeply.

"Aaah—" he sighed, drawing a chapped hand across his lips. "I'm on my way," he said jerkily, "for Morgan."

David, who had been on the floor pulling off John's socks, got to his feet. "Let me go," he begged. But Henry shook his head.

"No, you stay here. I can get George Morgan out when nobody else can." He looked down at John, then at me, and a flicker of exaltation passed over his tired face.

"He did it, Abigail. Licked 'em cold. Talked them right out of it. And they'd have done it, sure as creation. Get him to bed now." He seized the doorknob, a blast of icy air breathed through the room, and he was gone.

John opened his eyes, blinking at the light.

"Who . . . went . . . out?" he asked, his voice so weak I thought my heart would break.

"Henry. It was Henry, John," I managed to answer. "He's gone for George Morgan. You're done out."

A ghost of his old smile trembled across his white face. "Who? Me . . . done out? Not quite, girl. No sense dragging George out . . . night like this. . . ."

George Morgan came out of our bedroom and dropped into a chair beside the kitchen stove. Gim Lee gave him a cup of coffee, and he gulped it down noisily, handing it back for more. Gray dawn had come, but the snow was falling faster than ever. Gim Lee carved slices of ham and threw them into the sizzling pan. The kitchen was filled with the pleasant smell of their cooking. Henry nodded in a chair, David and Abby stood close together at the window, silently watching the winter day creep in. I rocked mechanically, listening consciously to the old chair's squeak.

"John's asleep," George said. "He'll stay like that for a while. Best we can do is leave him alone to do it." He looked about the room. "Somebody who knows might be kind enough to tell me what happened. All I can get is that John broke up an attempt to dynamite the aqueduct." He regarded Henry, sagging in his chair. "Wouldn't be a bad idea to pop *you* into bed, I'm thinking."

Henry's head jerked up and his eyes flew open. Bloodshot, they glared at Morgan. Then his chin sank slowly

162

to his breast again. George laughed. He turned to David. "How about it, young fellow? Any law against talking?"

David shook his head. "Not that I know of, sir," he said.

Abby sat on the arm of my chair, her hand finding mine.

"They were easy enough to find," David began. "They'd built a big fire and we could see it through the snow a long way. We could hear them, too—like a pack of coyotes, and somebody emptied a six-shooter."

I stopped rocking and felt Abby's warm fingers squeezing my cold hand.

"A little way off," David was saying, "Mr. Weston slowed down. He'd been in the lead. He said for us to take it easy from there—I couldn't see how they could hear us anyhow for all their whooping and yelling. But we did as Mr. Weston said, and came riding out of the snow smack up on 'em. Must have looked like spooks—three of us just suddenly appearing like that. It got so quiet all of a sudden you could hear the snow falling, I swear, and the fire snapping." We all sat tense and still, seeing the picture through David's words. "Somebody yelled. I saw maybe half a dozen—I reckon there must have been twenty-five or thirty there—slip away, out of the light, so we couldn't see what they were up to. Mr. Weston sort of stood up in the stirrups.

" 'Hello, boys,' he said, as natural as if he'd just dropped in to see what the noise and the fire were about. 'Having a little party?' he said.

"Nobody answered. You could hear a stick fall out of the fire and sizzle in the snow. There was the aqueduct levee stretching away on each side. Then, from way in

163

the back, somebody yelled out, 'What's it to you?' I looked where the voice came from, but they were packed too close to see. Besides, when we came up, nearly all of them had moved out between us and the fire. That made it hard to see, looking against the light like that. I felt Mr. Cabot's hand on my leg. Guess he was afraid I might start to do something rash."

Henry straightened and opened his eyes. Evidently he had been following the story as closely as any of us, though he had appeared to be asleep. "How'd I know what you'd do?" he demanded, blinking.

David paid no attention to the interruption.

"It didn't seem to ruffle Mr. Weston any," he went on. "He just settled back in the saddle and kept his hands crossed on the pommel."

"Kept 'em in sight," Henry explained, his eyes closing.

"Yes, sir. Mr. Weston looked around for a minute or so, and this same rough voice yelled out again, 'What's it to you?'

"Mr. Weston said, as good-natured as you please, that it was nothing, he guessed. Said he didn't recollect getting an invitation.

"You see," David explained earnestly, "Mr. Cabot and I were right alongside of him. That's why I didn't miss a thing that was said or done.

" 'Then why the hell don't you go on back where you come from?' this voice sings out.

"I still couldn't see anything, but quite a few of those in front turned around, and I heard somebody say something short, but couldn't make out what it was. The gang was starting to come out of that huddle. I didn't know what it meant, but it seemed that Mr. Weston did. 'Maybe I might go home,' he said, 'if I knew who wanted to get rid of me so much.'

"There wasn't any answer to that, but a couple more of the fellows sidled off into the dark. It didn't look so good to me." David paused, took a deep breath, and moved restlessly about the kitchen.

Abby's hand tightened on mine. George Morgan was drinking his fourth cup of coffee. Gim Lee had quietly slid the platter of ham into the oven and was listening intently. Of all this I was but vaguely conscious. I saw the picture David's words painted, but as though reflected in a dull mirror that blurred its contours. What I really saw—and vividly—was John, in the snow, facing the mob. I had to pull my mind back to David's words.

"It was about then that Harry Wilkins pushed his way through the crowd. Harry Brewer was with him. They came right up, and Brewer laid his hand on Lobo's neck— and Lobo didn't like it much. 'Why don't you go back home, John?' Brewer said. 'We got a job to do, and you can't stop us. No use having any trouble—and no use you getting mixed up in it.'

"Mr. Weston said, 'That's nice of you, Harry. But there's things you sometimes have to mix up in to keep others out of trouble.' I noticed he was leaning forward in the saddle, looking at a kind of lump, all covered with snow, in front of Lobo's forefeet. He swung out of the saddle and bent over and picked this bundle up, and when the snow fell

165

away, you could see it was a sack of something. Something lumpy. It was plenty quiet out there, now.

"Mr. Weston didn't take his eyes off of Brewer and the rest. He reached into the sack and brought out a stick of dynamite. By that time you could even hear the men breathing. Mr. Weston turned the thing over in his hand and sat there, studying it. I don't think a finger moved anywhere in the crowd. He nodded and put the stick back in the sack and dropped it easy into the snow again.

" 'Good powder,' he said, and looked around as if he'd said the snow might let up toward morning. 'Eighty percent,' he said. 'City powder, too. Ought to be good!'

"That went through Brewer like a needle. 'City powder, hell!' he squawked, but he didn't sound too brave. Harry Wilkins' mouth fell open and he looked downright scared. Brewer tried to bluster. 'I know where that powder come from,' he said.

"Mr. Weston just looked at him; then he reached down again and brought a stick out and handed it to him.

" 'You think you do,' he said. 'Take a good look at that. There's their mark—city of L.A.'

"Brewer looked like somebody had slugged him. He stood there staring at the thing for all he was worth. The rest crowded up, looking too. Then, quicker than it takes to tell it, Brewer and Wilkins were down on their knees, pulling sticks out of the sack and looking at them. Mr. Weston kept watching.

"Brewer let out a word I won't repeat here and straightened up. 'I never seen that powder before,' he said. 'That ain't what we had!'

166

"Mr. Weston said he knew they'd never seen it before, and he said he didn't know what powder they had seen, though. He gave 'em a good looking over and then pointed to the sack. 'Just the same,' he said, 'that *is* city stuff, boys —and I don't have to tell you having it puts you in a pretty bad hole. Am I right? You'd've blown the city's aqueduct sky-high and you'd've stolen the city's powder to do it. You'd have been up the creek without a paddle.'

"You could have heard a pin drop, then, in deep snow! Harry Brewer cursed again like fury and sort of croaked, 'What's it all about, John?'

"Mr. Weston didn't answer that one right away. He went on studying those silly-looking faces turned up gaping at him, the trick turned on them completely—and they didn't know how. . . ."

David held his hands over the stove, rubbing the fingers slowly. After a long sigh, he went on, "Mr. Weston let 'em have it straight, then. He said, 'There's people from down below, besides the city itself, that have money tied up here. You all know how somebody's been buying up these seepage-watered ranches. They're gambling the city will have to pay damages on 'em sooner or later.'

"He made it clear, letting everything he said soak in even on the stupidest ones there. 'This thing has cost the city more than they figured,' he said. 'They've got to have a bond election to get more money for water they've not seen. If they don't vote bonds, those fellows that have gambled up here will be left holding the sack. Their kind don't like that. According to my book,' Mr. Weston said, 'they figured that if we could be prodded into some real

167

violence up here—like what you boys were planning on doing tonight—the voters would get so riled at us they'd vote bonds for anything. I could be wrong, but I've got a hunch I'm not.'

"The bunch around the fire started whispering as soon as he stopped for breath, and Mr. Weston's voice cracked out like a whip. I admit I jumped nearly out of my skin, and so did some of those fellows. 'You boys are out here to blow up the city's aqueduct. You've got city powder to do it with. That'll prove the whole works on you! There'll be enough sticks lying around in the sagebrush to bring all the evidence they'll need. There are men planted right in your crowd ready to squeal on you. God Almighty, use your heads!'"

David shook his head slowly. "He stopped right there, and you could pretty near feel that gang thinking. Then Harry Brewer spoke up. He said, 'All right, John, you win. There ain't going to be no party tonight. You get along home and don't take no more chances. You been sick.'

"Mr. Weston swung up into his saddle again. I could see him smiling. . . ." David's voice broke, he swallowed. "He gathered up the reins and looked round at them and said, 'Anything else on your minds?'

"They thanked him then, the best they could—that tough bunch—" Admiration quivered in David's voice. "They started hollering out to him to take care of himself, and I swear some of them were even trying to shake his hand. It was a good ten minutes, I guess, before he could get free enough to rein Lobo round and head for home.

Right then is when I got scared. Something about . . . his face—it wasn't just right. . . ."

The passionate admiration that had illumined David's enthusiastic account died. His voice was flat and tired as he went on.

"We hadn't gone a hundred yards before Mr. Weston started to cough. I thought it'd tear him apart. I got my arm around him and Mr. Cabot poured some whisky down him. Then Mr. Cabot got *his* arm about him on the other side—and that's the way we got him home. I'll never forget those three miles!"

David slumped down at the table, burying his face in his arms. George Morgan went to him, touched his shoulder, and walked out of the kitchen without a word and toward the stairs that led to John's room.

Chapter 15.

*F*OR ten days John's life hung in the balance. Inflammation of the lungs set in and with it a raging fever. George Morgan came faithfully, sometimes reaching us in the middle of the night or the early morning hours. The terrible winter was taking its toll, and George was worked to distraction. He suggested a trained nurse, but I rejected this advice, maintaining that if I couldn't nurse my own husband I might as well be dead. I felt so vehemently about this that George gave in, although Abby argued on his side, insisting the strain would be too much for me.

"All right, then," she said at last, "I'll take turns with you, and Dave can run the business."

Between us and Gim Lee, who somehow managed to get along with no sleep at all, we nursed John through those dark ten days. David often came out to see how we were getting on. He looked much older and graver than the smiling young man who had come seeking hay for his horses. His face begged the questions he could not bring his lips to form. Seeing him so often there, Gim Lee chuckled irrelevantly. "Plitty soon wedding he come to this house."

Henry, who had moved in with us, was still full of the happenings of that awful night. "Nobody but John could have pulled it off," he declared. "That gang was primed for trouble. There were others among 'em besides valley boys, too."

I reminded him of David's having said he saw someone slip away into the darkness.

"That's right." He nodded emphatically. "I saw that, too. But I couldn't make out who they were. You know, I'd have been willing to swear I saw Little John in that gang. But just as I was nearly certain, somebody moved in the way and I never located him again. What the devil would *he* be up to?"

"Some of his Indian doings," I said, not very helpfully.

"I suppose so. Two or three years from now we may hear all about it if we're lucky," Henry added whimsically. "Two or three words at a time, too."

Joan, Carol, Mark, and Peter were in and out. If any mind had been less anguished over John I could have laughed at their awkwardness. They were so big and brawny, trying to walk softly in their high-heeled boots. City men came out as well—the engineers and Mr. Hooper, members of the committee, valley folk, all offering any assistance they might give.

On the tenth day John's fever subsided, and he drifted feebly out of the delirium in which he had mumbled about

171

his poplars drying up. I could hardly bear the glad burden of my joy as I looked into his eyes and saw them cleared of their torturing visions.

"Maybe I'd have done better to have listened to you, girl," he said that evening as I straightened his bed. "How long have I lain here like a useless log?"

"Ten days, dear." I felt so weak myself that I was obliged to sit down quickly on the edge of the bed. "But it's over now. You'll soon be all right again, John."

He nodded absently, and I saw his eyes go to the window. The day was sunny, only a few snow squalls gathering and breaking around Mt. Whitney. The snow marched down the Sierra and out onto the long slopes that swept up to them. Every pine and fir clung to its own crevice, standing sharp-etched and black against the white.

John moved his hand weakly toward the picture. "That's worth it, Abbie—worth fighting for, if you have to."

I couldn't stop the dry sob that broke on my lips. John's thin fingers groped for mine. "Stop that, Abbie. I'm here. Pretty much alive, too!"

"Yes," I choked. "But we didn't . . . know. . . ."

He reached up and stroked my hair, his hands tremulous but ever so tender. "Take it easy, girl. I'm hard to kill." He turned me toward him, but I was so blinded by tears that his face was only a blur. "You look beat out, completely."

"Beat out, nothing!" I protested. "Abby helped more than you'd believe possible, John, more than she'll ever know."

"Who's looking after her business?"

"David."

John laughed shortly. "It's in good hands. Judging by the way the lad looked after me that night, coming home, he knows how to meet an emergency."

"Don't talk about it," I urged, putting my hand on his lips.

"Don't or not, he managed very well," John insisted, "and I want to see him. I want to get those two in here together. I'm tired of all this dillydallying. Out of sheer stubbornness they're liable to miss something they can never replace."

"Well," I promised, to soothe him, "you shall get them together as soon as George Morgan gives the word."

John grinned at me and muttered something uncomplimentary to George. His face sobered, looking quite grim in its thinness and pallor. "Everything all right in the town, in the valley?"

"Oh, yes, dear," I answered too eagerly. "Everything is peaceful. David says Harry Brewer and Wilkins come into the office almost every day to ask for you. . . ."

"That's nice of 'em," John commented dryly. "Still, I don't know as I blame them too much for what they tried to do. They were stirred up—and not over nothing!" He lifted his head from the pillow to listen. "Who's that?" Someone was moving toward the room. I smelled coffee then. The door opened, and Gim Lee's grinning face appeared like a bright yellow moon above a heavily laden tray of food.

"You've brought enough to feed a lumber camp," I exclaimed; but John's grin broadened with anticipation as I

173

arranged the pillows behind him and drew my chair up so that I could feed him at least a portion of the bewildering array Gim Lee had prepared.

George Morgan rubbed his hands with satisfaction. "John's going to be all right," he beamed. "But he's got to lie low for a good long while. He needs rest more than anything. After a bout like his a relapse is no good. There are heart symptoms I don't like." He shot a quick look at me from under his heavy eyebrows. "Nothing to worry about, Abigail, provided he uses some horse sense. He's just got to take care of himself for a change. Natural enough in a man of his age. Keep him in bed as long as you can."

After three days, I let David into the room, and made Abby go up with him. John smiled happily at the sight of them, standing together a little sheepishly.

"Hello there, Dave," he greeted. "How's everything?"

"Couldn't be better, sir. It's good to see you. You gave us a scare, you know."

"A good thing, too," John chuckled. "Makes you all appreciate me more! Especially my wife. Still, I'm mightily obliged to you, young fellow."

"What for?" David asked innocently.

"Nothing much." John was elaborately casual. "Just riding out and facing that mob would seem a chore to some fellows. And holding me in the saddle all the way home wasn't too easy."

"It wasn't anything, sir," David insisted, but I saw Abby's

174

fingers touch his ever so lightly. I could not tell whether John had seen too. He only said with a twinkle,

"No. Practically nothing. But I'm obliged to you."

John's eyes roamed toward the window as they were so often doing, these days when he must lie in bed. It was snowing again, a wet, soggy, heavy-falling snow. His eyes dwelt somberly upon the forlorn bare branches of his poplars, then he drew his gaze away and looked into David's face.

"My wife tells me that with Abby playing nursemaid, you've been looking after Golden Valley Lands," he said.

"Yes, sir, that's right."

John looked from David to Abby, back to David again. "That makes you two partners, the way I see it."

"I wouldn't go so far as that," David answered plaintively, and I saw him squeeze Abby's clinging fingers. "The way I'm ordered around I figure I'm more of a hired man."

John raised himself on his pillows. "I won't argue that point. What I want to know is what damn' foolishness is keeping you two from the real partnership—for keeps, I mean?"

Both Abby and David blushed, then Abby burst out courageously, "I'll tell you, Grandpa! He thinks that because I have a little money of my own and he hasn't— and hasn't a job, either, as he says—or rather, he has a job and doesn't think it's one, or he thinks. . . ." She bit down hard on her lip and a sudden tear slid down her cheek. "Oh, I don't know *what* he thinks, and I don't care, either," she ended wildly.

David faced her, ominously quiet. "You know I want

to marry you. And you ought to have got it through your head that I won't until I can take care of you, Abby. I can't do that up here, and I can't quit here until this water fight is ended and I. . . ."

"Here, here, take it easy, son," John stopped him, half laughing. "I'd say neither one of you has a corner on damn' foolishness. You want me to get well quick? All right. Let me look forward to a first-rate wedding in this house. And soon, too. That's the only prescription that'll bring me up out of this bed in a hurry!"

His eyes dulled broodingly, and his voice suddenly sounded much weaker. "It'll take the curse off a lot of things, that will. L.A., for instance. Lawlessness. Injustice. Ranches drying up. Helpless people, ruined." Each word cost a painful effort, and I came forward, trying to hide my fear under efficient briskness.

"All right, dear," I said. "Don't talk any more now. We . . . we'll think about all you've been saying." I looked beseechingly at Abby and David. "You don't need to worry about them any more."

"No, indeed, Grandpa John," Abby said. "I'll raise Mr. Allen's pay. Then I'll march him over to the courthouse with a gun in his ribs till he buys a license."

"That's right." John's voice was scarcely more than a whisper. "See you do that. . . ." With a sigh like a tired child, he settled back on his pillow.

In the sitting room, near the window, Abby stood in the close circle of David's arm. She turned only her head as I came in.

176

"Isn't it wonderful, Hanny?" she cried, her eyes as full of joy as they had been of tears a few minutes ago.

"Of course, it's wonderful," I answered and kissed Abby, then David. But my thoughts had stayed in the bedroom with John. I was frightened at his sudden weakness and wondering if I should send for George Morgan.

"Did we tire him out, d'you think?" David asked anxiously.

I couldn't conceal my anxiety, but I tried to reassure those two. "I don't think so," I answered. "He's wanted so to talk to you. It's just that he hasn't his strength yet."

"And no wonder!" Abby slipped out of David's arm and moved nearer me. She looked uncertainly at David. "Ought we to bother Hanny with it now?" she asked.

"If it's important, yes," I said.

"I think it is," David stated firmly. "So does Little John. The last thing he said before we left this morning was to tell Mr. Weston if he was able. If not, to tell you, but no one else, not even Mr. Cabot."

I sat down. "Get on with it, David," I urged.

"Little John found this at the . . ." he hesitated—"the aqueduct the other night." He handed me a round tin box which I recognized as the container of percussion caps. On the cover was some partially erased lettering that might have been scraped off with a knife. Remaining were the letters "C" and "L.A." I opened the box gingerly. It was about two-thirds full of brass percussion caps. I looked up at David with a questioning, "Well?"

"Little John says he *saw* Bushnell give that fellow Rawlins a percussion cap box exactly like that. Harry Lee

177

and Hahn were with him at the time. All three will swear to it."

"They can't swear it was the same box," I pointed out.

"That's right," David agreed. "But remember the city dynamite that Mr. Weston and Mr. Cabot and I saw that night? Little John says he has twenty witnesses to prove that Rawlins was there. He swears Rawlins was the one that yelled out at Mr. Weston. Says he saw Rawlins hide something in a greasewood bush. Later Little John found that box in the very place, stuck away in the bush. He says he's got witnesses." David shrugged. "Maybe he has. If he hasn't, I'll bet on him to produce some. He claims he's pretty sure he saw Bushnell himself hanging around. I think he's got quite a case, Mrs. Weston."

I pushed my fear to the back of my mind. Even if all Little John saw were true, I thought, what good would it do? A man like Bushnell would produce a hundred perjured witnesses if he needed them. Then it would all too simply become the word of white men against that of Indians. . . .

"Why didn't Little John take all this evidence to the sheriff?" I asked. Yet I knew well enough that somewhere in Little John's mind lurked some crafty plan. He never forgot that, first, he was an Indian, and a white man only when it was more convenient to remember it.

David shook his head distractedly. "I don't know, Mrs. Weston. I suggested that the first thing, and I thought he was going to grab that box of caps and walk right out. He was obviously offended."

"Didn't you ask him why he objected?" I asked.

178

"Yes. He said for me to keep quiet and get MacAndrew up here right away."

"A lot of good that will do!" I exclaimed bitterly. "Your Mr. MacAndrew isn't going to like it that his beloved aqueduct missed being blown to perdition—missed by an eyelash, at that!"

"You bet he isn't! But he's going to be keener than a bird dog to find out who's responsible for the thing. It might give him the very opening he's looking for."

It was on the tip of my tongue to suggest that if Mr. MacAndrew needed any opening, Haiwee certainly supplied it, when I thought I heard a door closing very softly. It seemed to be at the back of the house, but that could hardly be since no one was in the house but us three and John, asleep upstairs. As it was a Sunday, Gim Lee had gone to town; I had seen him go before David and Abby came.

Full of anxiety for John as I was, the thought came to me that I might not have set the brick against his door, so that a draft could slam it shut. I hurried upstairs. From the top of the stairs I could see—and I gripped the banister, summoning all my strength in order to enter John's room. The door was wide open, the bedclothes thrown back, and the bed empty. John's dressing gown and slippers were nowhere to be seen.

Chapter 16.

ALTHOUGH I could dimly hear the pounding feet and excited voices, they had no meaning for me. One fact clamored over and over at my bewildered brain: I must find John.

I flew downstairs and out of the house. Hands plucked at me, but I brushed them aside. I was outdoors, running blindly through the snow and deepening dusk. A voice called shrilly, "John! John! John!," and it seemed a long time before I realized with a jar that it was my voice. Other voices mingled confusingly with it. Some forgotten, still feebly functioning corner of mind tried to tell me that Abby and David and Little John were calling too, searching too. But it was I who must find him.

I tripped over a snow-hidden root and sprawled my full length, only to scramble up and plunge on again. I felt no pain, only a mounting rage at the thing that had hindered my progress. I stumbled on, my breath stabbing at my lungs. Darkness dropped down as sudden and uncom-

180

promising as a black curtain. Snow fell on my bare head, stinging my cheeks, my eyelids, creeping chilly down my neck, but I forced my trembling legs on. Somewhere out in that cold and darkness and wet was John, sick, alone, out of his mind surely, needing me as he had never needed me before in all our life together.

I called and sobbed and prayed and struggled on. I seemed to be caught in impenetrable thickets. I stumbled to my knees, my hands and arms plunging into cold water that reached my elbows. And all the while the other voices were echoing about me. They seemed to be on every side. And above them all, beating solemnly against my ears, George Morgan's warning: "A relapse . . . heart symptoms I don't like. . . ."

Struggling to rise from the snow where I had stumbled, I felt the firm warmth of an arm about me. It was Abby's arm and her voice I heard, speaking quietly against my wet face, "Come, Hanny darling. You must come with me. Everything will be all right. You come back to the house."

The house! And John wandering through the night, perhaps dead in the snow? I tried violently to pull away; but as Abby clung to me, talking, soothing, holding me against her warmth and strength, my resolution failed, and I became a creature without will or thought or action of my own. Meekly, silently, I permitted Abby to lead me away from the frigid threatening dark, back to the warmth and light of my house.

"Everything will be all right," she kept saying soothingly. "Little John is here and Grampy and David and

181

Joe and Pete and Gim Lee. They will find Grandpa, Hanny. . . ." I could not hear the choke in her voice. "You'll only hurt yourself out here in the dark. Careful, dear—this ditch is where you fell before. That's it, step over like this. Poor darling, you're soaked to the skin, and so scratched and muddy. We'll have you warm and dry in a minute. . . ."

I blundered dully after her, led by the hand.

"Gim Lee's got bricks heating," she explained simply, "and we'll get the old hotwater bottle. . . ."

Something seemed to come alive at that, and I pulled and struggled to get away, outraged at this pampering while John. . . .

"Now, now, darling," Abby's arm tightened about me, and I saw the yellow light stream out from the kitchen door. Someone threw it wide and we stumbled in, Abby literally holding me up on my numb feet.

The light blinded me, yet I sensed that the room was crowded with people. As my vision slowly cleared, I saw Henry and Little John standing straight and quiet by the stove, and scattered about the room were Carrol, David, Joe Ramirez, and Pete. Joe's lips and hands moved constantly before his face and breast. Gim Lee was busy with great pots of water, some of them already steaming. Anger twisted me. What were they doing? Why weren't they looking for John? I clutched at Henry.

"Where is John?" I cried. "Why aren't you out hunting for him?"

The room seemed to stop breathing. Henry took my hands and held them tightly, but his eyes shifted away

182

from mine as I had never seen them do. Mark and Peter tiptoed in from somewhere else in the house. Horror such as I had not yet felt stabbed me. I saw Joan in a far corner, her face buried in her hands, little whimpers seeping through her fingers. My terror mounted.

"John!" I cried, struggling to free myself from Abby and Henry.

I was moving painfully toward the door, Abby and Henry supporting me. Down the miles of hallway, up more miles of stairs we crept, for my nightmare was still upon me. We reached the room John and I had shared for so long, and I saw through a dull mist the still form upon the bed.

Slowly, the mist cleared away and I pushed Henry and Abby from me. They gave in, at last, stepping back, stepping out of my consciousness, and I dropped to my knees, reaching for John's hand. I drew it close to me, seeking to warm it at my breast. Fumblingly, I slipped my other hand beneath John's head that lay so still upon the pillow. I knew then the truth. It was here before me in this figure so beloved, now so cold and still.

Gently, I laid John's head back upon the pillow. I folded the thin, veined hands across his breast. I got slowly to my feet, knowing that half of me had died. Wide-eyed, tearless, I turned to those who had brought me to this room. Others had followed, and I seemed to stare out over a multitude, all stricken with grief of their own and a share of mine. It was David who told me what I sought to know.

"We found him, Hanny, at the big sluice gate." Dully, uncaring, I yet noticed that he used Abby's name for me, as tenderly as she could have done. "You know—where

183

you turn the water along the poplars." His voice broke. "He . . . he'd managed to get it open."

It took the strength of two men to move that gate, even when there was no ice on the bank to grip it. . . .

"We . . . we think it was his trees. You know how it . . . it preyed on his mind. Opening the gate must have done something to . . . to his heart. He was lying. . . ." David choked, turned, and pushed his way through the group and out of the room.

I stood motionless, and the vision passed with a strange clarity before my blurred eyes. I saw John struggling with the water-logged gate, saw him slip and fall, struggle to his feet again to wrestle with the gate until at last it swung free, beaten by the spurious strength of his delirium. I could hear the water rustling down the cold, dry ditch, bearing the dead leaves before it. . . .

"Could you, please, leave me a little?" I said.

I kept my vigil. Not by the bed but beside a window in my little sitting room. I could breathe and think and move. But I was dead as a stone. My eyes strained out into the darkness toward those things we had built together— orchards, meadows, fences, and barns. Beyond them rose the mountains we loved, the hills from whence came our strength so often, the lines of brown willows descending to our possessions. And back there, brooding, waiting where we had thrust it, lay the desert. Though I could not see them now, John's poplars stood about our land, the trees he had loved so much and died for. How often I
184

had watched the lyrical movement of their branches reaching toward the clouds.

After a little, one by one, those others who loved John came tiptoeing in, all except Little John whom he had called son. Each sought in his own way to bring a little comfort. I answered them, I touched their hands, but I knew neither their words nor my own. Later, perhaps, when the mind emerged from its shock of grief both paralyzing and protective, these words would register and have meaning. Now they fell upon my numbed spirit with the hollowness of mockery. Quiet, anxious, sorrowful, they came and went, till only Abby was left, sitting on the floor very close to me, her hand clinging fast to mine.

"Hanny," she breathed, when we had sat in silence I do not know how long, "Look!"

Far out on the desert blossomed a pinprick of red. It was joined by another, another, and another, till a host of these points of fire lighted the desert sky in a straight long row leading to the east.

"The Joshuas! They're burning the Joshuas for Grandpa, Hanny. . . ."

Watching, I came alive again. My heart leaped in answer to the leaping flames. Down that blazing road my John would ride until he came to the gates of that Other Place. It was so clear to me that I could see it.

I drew Abby's bright head against my knee, and felt the terrible walls of my sorrow break and crumble as we wept together.

Chapter 17.

*T*HERE were some, as always, who took a somber pride and a dark comfort in the hushed throngs that came to do honor to John's memory. They called it the greatest funeral Golden Valley had ever known. I scarcely knew whether the crowd was great or small. My heart was in that grave where my loved one lay; and when they had filled it in, my thoughts clung with the upflung poplars that guarded it, those friends he had cared for through so many seasons.

When it was over, Will stayed with me a little while.

"They broke the mold after they made him," he said, and that was the only time during the tragic day I cried.

"You looked so tiny," Abby told me, averting her face so I might not see her own fresh tears. "So straight and proud and brave." She touched her cheek against my hair. "MacAndrew was there," she added hesitantly. "He'd asked Dave about the propriety of his coming to the funeral." She paused again, then went on resolutely,

"David says Mr. MacAndrew was hard hit. He had beautiful things to say about Grandpa John."

I closed my eyes sharply for a moment, thinking that fine words came most easily when they came too late.

"He did send a beautiful floral offering, Hanny. So did David's friends and those engineers who used to visit Grandpa."

I remembered them, slow-spoken, quiet men, lean and weathered. John had enjoyed their visits, but I could not help thinking of them now as city men. They and their kind had caused John's death. Abby must have seen the bitterness in my face, for a sorrowful look touched her and she said pleadingly, "Don't be this way, Hanny darling. So . . . apart from everybody and everything. Grandpa wouldn't want it, would he? He . . . he'd want all of us to go right on where he left off and . . . and finish the work he began. Isn't that so, dear?" She touched my folded hands.

I sat, turning her softly spoken words over in my mind with painful effort. I knew she was right. At last I said humbly, "Thank you, child."

I tried to pick up the scattered threads, to weave them into some pattern that would serve those I loved. I puttered about endlessly, doing small tasks that would as well have been left undone. I found my crochet work and busied my restless fingers with it hour after hour. No one would ever use the botchy, crude edging that emerged from the needle, but it served its purpose.

The nights were worst. I read till the gray morning hours

187

came, and my eyes burned and rebelled, and I would have to lay my book down without a notion as to what I had read. The bed, once shared with John, seemed now so wide I could not bear it, and I made the couch up in my little sitting room and passed my few hours of oblivion there.

Then one day I caught David Allen looking anxiously at me, and when I returned his look, he fidgeted a little and burst out, "Mr. MacAndrew has been up."

I tightened inwardly, not recognizing the first sign of returning interest in what went on about me.

"Abby, Little John, MacAndrew, and I had a long session," he went on, "about that attempted dynamiting. We showed him a couple of sticks of the dynamite Little John had got hold of, and the caps. We showed him the confessions, too."

His first words had been rather meaningless to me, but at this point something seemed to burst in my brain and I cried out sharply, "Confessions? What confessions?"

"Bushnell's and Rawlins'," David said simply.

"You have confessions from that pair?" I asked unbelievingly. "How did you get them? What's in them?"

"Little John got them," David said. "Don't ask me how, for I don't know. As to what's in them, just about everything."

"Tell me, David," I demanded, almost excitedly. "Tell me everything."

"Well, there's their part in stirring up the trouble. They did most of the burnings, and engineered the plot to dynamite the aqueduct. And plenty about the clique that

188

was buying up seepage ranches, too. They didn't miss much."

"Where are they?" I found I was actually trembling with interest.

"Who? Bushnell and Rawlins? Or the confessions?"

"Both," I answered impatiently. I had a sudden desperate desire to hold those confessions in my hands, to crucify with them every city man who had had any part in our misery.

"Bushnell and Rawlins are gone," David stated flatly. "For good, probably."

I leaned forward hopefully. "Have you the confessions with you?" I demanded.

David crossed the room to the fireplace and leaned against the mantel. He stood there a while without saying anything. At last he answered briefly, "I haven't them. MacAndrew has."

I stared at him incredulously. To surrender such a weapon to MacAndrew seemed nothing short of madness. "What do you mean?" I whispered.

"Just what I say, Mrs. Weston." His tone was dogged, his jaw set. "We didn't just jump, or get tripped into it. We had Will Fiske down and all five of us talked it over —plenty! Mr. Fiske seemed a bit doubtful about what use we could make of what we had. Technically the confessions weren't too perfect, perhaps—not as legal evidence. But they were *true*. That we knew."

"How?"

David thought for a moment and then evaded the question. "You'll understand, Mrs. Weston, when Little John tells you the story."

"Little John?"

David nodded. "The point now is that the facts we got down on paper can be mighty useful to MacAndrew. And to us later. We talked it all over and Mr. MacAndrew thought that with those confessions and some other facts he'd gathered himself, he could force through a settlement on the seepage lands. Fiske and Little John agreed with him."

"Which won't bring the dead to life," I said dully, unable to help myself.

"No," David's voice was gentle. "But neither. . . ."

"Will the confessions in my hands," I answered for him. "You do trust MacAndrew implicitly?"

He met my gaze. "I do," he said. "Absolutely."

"I think . . . John would have, too," I said, and turned my eyes toward the desert.

Little John listened stolidly as I hurled questions at him.

"Oh," he said at last, as though light were just dawning behind his inscrutable dark eyes. "You want to know about Bushnell and Rawlins?"

I closed my eyes. For the past fifteen minutes I had been working toward nothing else.

"I guess maybe they thought they'd better talk." He lifted a shoulder.

"Little John," I said, carefully curbing my impatience, "I want to know *how* you obtained those confessions. I want to know *what has become of those two men.*"

190

He looked at me blankly. "They went away," he said.

Each of his evasive, brief answers fired my need to know what really had occurred, and I determined to find out no matter what it took. I said, carefully choosing my words, "There's something I want to say to you, Little John, something I should have said long ago, maybe. Now listen.

"You and I have been very close, closer perhaps than Mark and I. That is because we have always understood one another so well, for one thing. For another, it is because I promised your father when you were a newborn babe that I would be a mother to you. I have never demanded anything of you, Little John. I don't now. But if you'd have me sleep nights, tell me all you can of this matter. . . ."

He stared at me in his odd way for a full moment, then to my surprise, he reached over and touched me upon the shoulder just as Joaquin Jim had done that night in the smoke-filled hogan when I first took Little John into my arms.

"You're scared on my account what happened to those fellows?" he asked. I only nodded. Now that I was close to learning the truth I was, perversely, not at all sure that I wanted it. Something in the Indian's manner made me shrink from knowledge.

"We rounded 'em up, Harry Lee, Hahn, Injun Joe, me. We took 'em out to a rancheree. I'd sent the people away." He paused to roll a cigarette, and I could imagine what a quartet they had made for those two miserable wretches to face in a lonely rancheree. Four pure Indians with an

Indian's indifference to cruelty should cruelty serve a purpose. . . .

"They didn't want to go much," Little John said, watching the blue smoke curl upward. A reminiscent smile touched his lean lips. "It was raining pretty hard. Pretty cold, too. Hard for a man afoot to keep up with a fast-walking horse. All my horses walk pretty fast."

Instantly I knew what he meant, what form of torture they had used to obtain the confessions from the men they had watched and suspected and knew to be guilty. My heart gave a sick plunge as again my imagination vividly painted the picture for me. A man, hands tied, a riata about him taut to the fast-stepping horse. A man in such predicament will trot, run, anything to keep going, for if he falls he will be dragged without mercy. The wild clutching at the tight rope, the fighting for one—just one —little foot of slack. Men had died dreadfully under this torture, their last desperate cries smothered in mud and desert gravel.

"It wasn't very bad," Little John answered my sick look. "Maybe four-five miles." Four or five miles like that on a bitter night, stumbling and falling, scrambling up only to stumble again, to keep going or die, and the riata never slackening an inch. For all the evil they had wrought, a measure of the punishment due that pair had overtaken them that rainy night.

"I let 'em thaw out," Little John said calmly. "Then we talked. They didn't want to much. They changed their minds." Little John blew a succession of fine smoke rings above his head. "Rawlins changed first. Bushnell's tougher.

He didn't like what Rawlins was saying. He said so. Injun Joe shut him up." A reddish light glowed for a second in Little John's eyes.

"Rawlins wrote down what he said, and I kicked him out. He's a bum. The other fellow wasn't easy. Wasn't deaf, either."

"Not deaf? How did you find that out?"

"Lots of little things that happened. That night at the Ditch I sneaked up behind him and did this." Little John pulled out his jackknife and clicked the blades twice. The sound was very like that of a pistol being cocked. "He spun around just like he was shot. That's when I knew for sure. At the rancheree I yanked that tin thing off his ear. He stuck it out for a long time. But pretty soon he started to talk. He's tough, all right." Little John spoke respectfully for the moment. "It took longer than I figured it would. You don't want to hear that part of it."

I drew a deep breath. No, I didn't want to hear that part. As from far away, I heard Little John's expressionless voice.

"After a while we got to the country road. At the county line."

I knew the place with its weathered board sign, "Inyo County" on the one side, "Kern County" on the other. On either side of the road wastes of sagebrush spread drably.

"I told him to get going and keep going," Little John said. "Not to never come back. Never. He blubbered some —but he got. I watched him till he was out of sight."

He rolled and lighted another cigarette.

"He didn't look like much. You wouldn't have thought

he could hurt anybody." He grunted, Indian fashion. "Little feller, bent over, limping down a wet road." He half turned his body, looked directly at me. Again, briefly, his strange eyes glowed.

"You thought maybe I killed him?"

"I didn't know," I whispered.

"Ugh! I didn't need to. I'd just as soon. He helped kill Uncle John."

He touched me again on the shoulder, gently, with his long forefinger. Then he slipped noiselessly from the room.

Chapter 18.

ABBY had made an appointment with me for eleven sharp in her office. I did not know what it was about, for whenever I asked a question all I could extract from her was an impish smile and the one word, "Surprise!" Little John drove me in, and was very prompt, but I was not, keeping him waiting for the better part of half an hour. I had fallen into this bad habit since John's going—wasting time on foolish waverings and indecisions.

It was after eleven-thirty when we drove into Independence. Little John opened the door for me, and I stepped into the warmth of Abby's little office to find it filled with people, all of whom seemed at first glance to be strangers. I drew back timidly. But even as I hesitated, I saw David Allen smiling at me from over Abby's shoulder, and Will Fiske on her other side, and Harry Lee at his table. I began to sort out the other faces, too: MacAndrew's, Hooper's, the City Attorney's. The others were strangers, well groomed and bearing the unmistakable mark of city living.

With Little John's hand under my elbow, I moved forward, bowing to Mr. MacAndrew and Mr. Hooper. I smiled at Abby, David, Will, and Harry. I heard myself apologizing for my tardiness, but Mr. MacAndrew was bowing over my hand, assuring me that their time was mine. He began a series of introductions, the first to Mayor McPhail.

"Anither Scot," MacAndrew said gravely, "albeit mixed with the Irish which does na lend itself to stabeelity."

A subdued laugh traveled round the office.

Next came the City Attorney, a Mr. Bolton, tall, sallow, and hawk-faced. I remembered having seen, and instantly disliking him in Charlie Hunter's courtroom.

"We pay him to keep us out of trouble," MacAndrew rumbled. "Thus far he has na done too weel."

When I had met them all, MacAndrew looked gravely at me for a long moment.

"I'll no burrden ye with mere worrds, ma'am," he broke his silence. "But I'd hae ye know here and the noo that I grieve wi' ye in your ain grief. I hae known many men in my life. I hae known none finer than John Weston."

My heart tightened, seeing Angus MacAndrew in that moment for what he was; and I was ashamed of the bitterness I had harbored against him for so long.

"The noo," he continued briskly, "we're here on a business that I hope we can come to agreement on. Agreement that will be to the advantage of both parties—Golden Valley and our city."

The room was so still after this speech that I could hear the flutter of flames in the old potbellied stove at the back of the office. I looked at Abby, then Will, then David—but vainly. Their blank faces told me nothing. I turned again to MacAndrew and waited.

"Without beating around the bush," he went on, "we've come to see what arrangement we can reach regarding this Haiwee matter."

It had come, then, what John had so often called the break. Thanks mainly to Will Fiske, we had outwitted the city, and thanks also to Little John and Abby. . . . But there must be more to it than that. My mind flew to the evidence Little John had gathered together against Sayville's man Bushnell, evidence they had turned over to MacAndrew for his own use. The cards were in our hands now, I thought, scarcely daring to believe it.

"That there might be no misunderstanding," MacAndrew went on heavily and carefully, "His Honor, Mayor MacPhail, most of the City Council, members of the Water Committee, our City Attorney, and others are here. 'Tis all in the open now, ma'am." A cold glint came into his shrewd eyes. "There is one ye'll note who is not present. I'm referring to former commissioner Sayville.

"Now that you're forewarned," a smile flickered across his ruddy face, "I'll turn further dealings over to Mayor McPhail."

McPhail smiled and shook his head. "No," he declined. "It's your party, Mac. Go ahead."

"Verra well," MacAndrew nodded. "We've come to ask your price for Haiwee." He hesitated, looking at me

197

sharply. "Ye understand, ma'am, that the city must hae it."

There was a silent stir, and the City Attorney's face darkened. I looked at Abby and Will again. I was being asked *my* price on Haiwee. As far as the world knew, the corporation, Golden Valley Lands, owned Haiwee, not I. Mention had not been made that I had any connection with the company. Of a sudden I was terrified of taking some false step, of saying what I should not say.

In the midst of my engulfing fear, Abby stepped forward, looking young and slim and out of place in this gathering of hard-bitten business men.

"It's all right, Hanny," she assured me. "Mr. MacAndrew knows all about the company, and you and the fund."

"I told him," Will Fiske supplied calmly.

"And a verra grand thing it was, too," MacAndrew said.

I suspected there were others in that room who did not think it at all a grand thing. But I strove to marshal my thoughts so that I might do as John would have me do. I forgot everything else, thinking only of John, longing for his guidance. I wished for it so intently that it actually seemed as though he were there, counseling me what to say. It was as though he were reminding me of what was at stake, of all that depended upon my answer now.

I saw again the strained, anxious faces at the Independence meeting. I saw these same people in Charlie Hunter's courtroom. I saw again the line before the closed doors of Frank Master's bank. I knew I must not make a mistake, Upon the gold that Uncle Amos had left me and the use we had made of it, rested the future of so many people, their happiness, their lives. They must not suffer through a woman's weakness. And suddenly I felt sure of myself.

The men in Abby's office were looking at me, waiting for what I would say.

"Yes," I heard my own voice saying quietly without a trace of the terror that had beset me, "we will sell you Haiwee. But upon what you may regard as harsh terms."

"We're no here to quibble," MacAndrew answered at once. I caught a flash of hostility in Mr. Bolton's eyes.

"First," I said, feeling my way, but with new certainty, "Golden Valley Lands is to be reimbursed for what it paid for Haiwee. Second"— I looked about the ring of avid faces—"full compensation must be made to those who have suffered damage by reason of your activities, and to those whom you will damage in the future."

I settled back in the rocking chair Abby had put in this shabby little room for me, long ago. Street sounds came in, the grind of wagon wheels, the clop-clop of horses' hoofs, the click of boot heels upon board walks, the staccato cough of a cold automobile starting. Inside the office, the silence stretched and stretched.

"Hard terms indeed, Mrs. Weston." It was Mayor McPhail who spoke at last. "And unpredictable."

"Impossible!" Mr. Bolton spat out, sitting upright.

"No harder than you have been to us, Mr. McPhail," I said inexorably. "No more impossible, Mr. Bolton, than it has been for seepage ranchers to live with their water supply cut off."

"Water they never owned," snapped Bolton.

"But that they've used without question for forty years," Will Fiske retorted.

Again there was silence. I wondered if we had come to an impasse. Through my mind swept visions of the ruined, dying ranches, the faces at our meetings, Fred Lindstrom's homesick letters, the pathetic line before the bank waiting for the opening of doors that would never open again, Jane Calkins sweating in someone's kitchen—John, lying so still in our room while the Joshuas flamed across the desert.

"Acceptance lets Los Angeles in for commitment to pay out unknown and unlimited sums," Mr. Bolton said grimly. "We would be guilty of breach of faith to the taxpayers. I advise fighting it out."

"Goin' to yon taxpayers wi' certain matters o' which we are conversant, dootless?" MacAndrew said coldly. "Askin' for more money, wi' not a drop o' water flowin'? I dinna think the people will like that overmuch. I dinna think they'll find water that's brewed from tears o'er pleasant to the taste."

"It's not so great a problem, after all," Will put in. "You know about what you're going to do, and where." He looked at MacAndrew.

"Aye. Within bounds."

"Then why not have a commission appointed? You pick one, we'll pick one. The two will select a third. They can determine what lands will be affected and what not, and fix amount of damage."

"And who would their decisions be binding upon?" Mr. Bolton demanded.

Will shrugged. "No one perhaps. But once damages were fixed by such a body, I'd defend the city gratis against demands for more. Besides, you've always the right of condemnation."

A babel of talk broke out—objections and questions raised, answered, or left unanswered. The clamor tired me so that I closed my eyes. Then I realized that Mayor McPhail was addressing me directly.

"You realize that your plan involves many technicalities, Mrs. Weston?" he asked. "Enabling ordinances must be passed. Money must be made available, a commissioner selected and his powers defined. All that and more. Also, there will be taxpayers to be informed. They may have their say at the next election," he added dryly. "If we accept in principle, you'll understand there'll be delays?"

"I can see that Mrs. Weston is getting tired," Will Fiske said abruptly. "She's had enough to go through. We can escrow our side of the deal with your instructions for completion when you have taken the necessary legal steps."

"Which will be no easy matter," Attorney Bolton snapped.

"Easier than to see this Sayville mess in the newspapers," MacAndrew responded. This evoked another gust of words until the mayor put an end to it.

"The thing's settled," he said crisply. "So far as is within my present power, Mrs. Weston," he added turning politely to me, "I accept your terms on behalf of the city. Mr. Fiske and Mr. Bolton can work out the details. It will take time, but I promise that there will be no undue delay."

"A promise which I second," MacAndrew rumbled.

201

"Those who have been hurt will be cared for," the mayor continued. "And as to the gentlemen who planned to profit from the seepage lands, there are some I suspect will be turning them back to their owners rather than get acquainted with San Quentin. The information you gave MacAndrew"—he smiled a little—"was most helpful. It was an Indian who worked for you, was it not?"

"My foster son," I replied coldly. "He does his own thinking and has his own ways of finding out what he needs to know."

"No doubt of it." McPhail's tone made me wonder how much he actually knew. "At the City Hall we could do with men like him."

When the others had bid me goodbye, I found Angus MacAndrew bending over me, speaking very quietly in his deep voice which could be very gentle indeed.

" 'Tis been a long road, ma'am, and darkened by many a shadow. There were times I wished I had never set eyes on your Golden Valley, as you well know, and times when I didna think the right way of doing things would ever win. And I am sure there were times when you doubted me sore. I'm hopin' that's forgotten now."

He pressed my hand and was gone. I had had no word for him, and I had none even for Abby's excited chatter when all the cars had driven away and we of the valley were left together. I was weary, an old woman, drained and empty. But it seemed still that John was near, trying to remind me of something he wanted done—something deeply important that he had urged on me before he went away. Abby, David, and Will were standing at the win-
202

dow, and as I looked at them I knew what it was that John had wished.

I beckoned to Will. As he listened to my whisper, his first startled look mellowed into a prodigious grin that cleft his ruddy face.

"Of course!" he agreed with enthusiasm. "That's something that's needed doing for a long while." He looked at his watch. "I could probably get him here in fifteen minutes, but I do think we ought to have Joan and Henry. Little John could run out to Manzanar and have them back in a couple of hours. In the meantime I'll talk to Charlie Hunter. I've an idea Charlie'd rather do this than any job of work he ever did."

My heart went out warmly to Will. What a good, loyal friend he had been through the years. I laid a grateful hand upon his arm, not trusting myself to speak, and at once he had Little John in the back room and was whispering to him. Little John's eyes met mine as he dashed out the door.

"What's all this whispering?" Abby demanded.

Before I answered her, I beckoned David to join us. "The 'books' you have talked so much about are balanced now," I said when they stood together before me. "Whatever comes to the valley, at least its people will be cared for. There is no need to wait any longer."

"Wait? Wait for what, Hanny?"

"For the wedding your grandfather wanted so much, my dear. We can have it for him right now, right here in your office. I . . . I'm sure he'll know. As soon as your mother and Henry get here, I want you two to be married, just as your Grandpa John wanted you to be."

Abby was staring at me with a starrier look than I had ever seen in her blue eyes. David went red, then white, his eyes full of startled rebellion that ebbed into uncertainty, then a half shamefaced joy that did my heart good.

"It's not only that your grandfather wanted it," I went on. "I've wanted it as much as he did. Call it selfishness, David, if you like. With all the changes that are coming I need a man to manage things for me. And then, too, handling Golden Valley Lands is no job for a woman. Is it, Abby?"

"Well. . . ." Abby murmured, glancing from under her eyelashes at David. "This isn't exactly what I thought. Oh, Hanny, I ought to. . . ."

Then she was in David's arms, all three of us close to tears of happiness when Will stormed in.

"Weddings," he observed, "do the cussedest things to ordinarily intelligent people. However, we can't even have one to cry over unless the groom gets to work. Quick, too."

David drew his arms reluctantly from about Abby. "So long as I can't get out of it," he said gaily, "tell me what's wanted."

"There's a stodgy old rule," Will answered, "about having a license to make these little matters legal. So I expect you'd better step along about it before Little John gets back."

They looked very straight and gallant, standing before Charlie Hunter, and somehow he managed to make the ceremony there in the dusty little office as grand as though it were held in a cathedral. I knew from Abby's radiant face that she was not even regretting the absence of wedding gown or bouquet, and David looked every bit as ecstatic though still a trifle dazed.

Little John was best man and Henry gave the bride away, not troubled by stage fright as he surely would have been in different surroundings. I sat in the old rocker and watched because I was wholly unable to stand on my two feet. I saw but dimly, too, because of the mist across my eyes. My heart nearly stopped its beating as the words reached my ears, "For better, for worse, in sickness and in health . . . until death do us part."

It was the ring John had placed on my hand so long ago that David Allen slipped on Abby's finger; and when it was done, they came to me, still hand in hand, kissing me even before they had embraced each other. The warmth of my love for them nearly overwhelmed me as I put my arms about them both.

Then Charlie Hunter warned sternly that the one decree of his court that was never to be set aside was that the groom should kiss the bride, and the little wedding party broke into a great confusion of gaiety and noise. Gim Lee, who had got into his best blue serge suit and come along with Joan and Henry, grinned without ceasing. He kept darting about the office, shaking hands with himself and saying, "You betcha, me fixee!" Little John's smile was the broadest I had ever seen on his enigmatic face. And Harry Lee, solemnly congratulating the couple, said to Abby, "I guess you won't need me any more for a bodyguard."

As I sat there basking in the happiness about me, the dingy walls of the little office seemed to melt away. It was as though I had only just come to Golden Valley, lying between its snow-capped mountains. I thought of the plowing of our first furrow and of my burning wish to have it straight and true. I remembered the cold, lumpy earth, and again felt it crumble in my chapped fingers. . . .

With a start, my mind came back to the office, and my fingers fumbled at the front of my dress. They found the little clasp and unpinned the old brooch. I beckoned to Abby, and as she knelt beside me, I pinned the brooch to her dress. I saw the tears spring to her eyes, and she caught my hand up, covering it with kisses.

"A gift for your wedding day," I said. "Should the time ever come when there are no more furrows in Golden Valley, at least you may cherish this earth from our first plowing."

2989